To my son Luke
with love and gratitude

One

It's weird how one tiny event can change your life forever. Like a sperm and an ovum getting it together. After that, one thing leads to another like some chain reaction. For years I'd reckoned my mother was past having babies. She seemed to have sorted out the messy connections between sex, reproduction and love. It hadn't occurred to me that she was capable of doing two at the same time. Not since I was born. I like to think those three things came together when I was conceived. I like to think she loved my father back then.

She certainly didn't love my stepfather, Trevor, when she fell pregnant with Kevin. At least, it wasn't recognisable as love. That's something I hadn't worked out, why people stayed together when they hated each other so much. Then Kevin was conceived, which I think was as much a shock to them as it was to me. But my mother recovered quickly. For a while she seemed to get a new lease on life.

"It's nice to know the old ovaries are still functional," she said, beaming like a young girl. "I thought that I'd wrecked them with years of contraceptive abuse."

Her good mood didn't last. As she got heavier and her belly and varicose veins began to swell, she became more and more uncomfortable and bad tempered. "I'm too old for this!" she'd freak at Trevor and me. "I can't make babies and beds and food and go out into the world to make money while you guys sit on your butts watching TV!" A bit unfair, as I was cramming for matric, and Trevor worked long hours as a mechanic. Not that I would ever stick up for Trevor, but my mother was impossible. Even then there was no way I could see which line of dominoes was going to fall next. Trevor certainly didn't. Maybe my mother didn't either. Not then.

Some people have wondered how I got so involved with something that wasn't exactly my problem. But I was involved right from the beginning. They weren't there when Kevin first stuck his head out into the world. It's not something you get over easily.

It was a Monday afternoon, and my mother was flopping around the house, hot and restless. She complained that the baby was hot and restless too, which made her feel worse and behave worse. She kept picking on me as though it were my fault the baby was a week late.

"It's thrown everything out!" she moaned, heaving her impossibly huge belly out of one chair, straining her way across the room, one hand pressed to her back, then dumping back down on to the sofa. "This is the worst day of my life!"

I'd heard that complaint many times before in a variety of contexts, so it didn't bother me. In any case, I was busy trying to cram two billion facts into what was left of my brain in time for the last matric exam the next day.

"I guess we both kinda leave things to the last minute," I said, trying to recall the life cycle of a mosquito.

"It's not me, Davey!" objected my mother. "It's this baby."

I studied her mountainous belly. Baby. I was still struggling to come to terms with the fact that there was some life form in there, something related to me via the vagaries and disasters of my mother's life.

It was then that she felt it, the first sign. "It's coming!" she gasped, a peculiar mixture of terror and relief on her face.

"Oh, no!" I leapt out of my chair. "Just wait!" I said. "Don't do anything! I'll phone Trevor!" He worked at a garage a couple of suburbs away.

My mother waved away any such suggestion.

"Don't bother yet," she said. "It takes hours for a baby to come out. With you it took twenty! That was only a twinge. Wait till it really gets going, I won't even be able to speak."

I looked at her doubtfully. In the eighteen years I'd known her, my mother had never been at a loss for words, not under any circumstances. But she *had* been known to miscalculate things. Like the time we were supposed to be going on holiday to Victoria West of all places, and it was only when we hit Springbok that she realised she'd taken the wrong turning three hundred kilometres back. That was the beginning of the end of the relationship with her third boyfriend since my dad, and *that* was several boyfriends back.

She seemed to be quiet for the moment, so I turned to my biology books again.

"I think I'll go and have a long slow bath," my mother said. "When Trevor gets in he can take me up to the hospital, if this isn't a false alarm."

I was glad to be alone and undisturbed for a while, and took the opportunity to revise the section on human reproduction, seeing the subject had come up. It's quite amazing, actually. I can't help feeling totally astonished by the way it all works. I don't think I could've thought it up myself. It'd be a perfect system if people weren't involved. And if it wasn't so wasteful. All those billions of sperm and hundreds of eggs in a lifetime. It's incredible that, what with the whole thing designed to produce babies as often and as efficiently as possible, my mother has only had two children in all this time. Contraceptives obviously work. Except when you don't use them. Like with Kevin and me. We're two more examples of her miscalculations, I reckon.

Or maybe I was the most calculated thing she ever did. Not then. It must've been a shock to her to fall pregnant at the age of sixteen. But I've come in useful. I've been the one male in her life that's stayed constant. I've never left her, not like the others. And what would she've done with Kevin without me?

Looking over my biology notes, I knew I would've taught it differently. Our teacher, she pretended she had it under control, but you could see it in her eyes. She was terrified to teach the subject to a whole room full of hormone-driven adolescents. You could see she couldn't wait to get on to something safe, like wind pollination.

I suspected that while her head and the curriculum said she must teach it, her heart said if you even mention the word sex, it turns people into raving maniacs that go out and fornicate with the first person they meet. I mean, none of us would have existed without sex, and the first thing any of us saw when we came into this world was our mother's vagina. Except for those poor sods born by Caesarean. That's a real deprivation, I reckon, not to come out the way you went in.

You see, you've got to start where people are at. I reckon that at puberty, when your body's going crazy, and pushing out all over the place, hair, boobs, dick, Adam's apple, it's kinda obvious that's where people are at. The body. We all sit in class, thinking about bodies and sex, and all the while Mrs Burnell is talking about reproduction as though it's an alien life form.

I'd be a good teacher. In fact, I'd be good at most things. Actually, I was really proud of myself that day Kevin was born. At the time I almost panicked, but now I think I handled it all amazingly.

I suddenly realised that it was getting late, and my mother hadn't come out of the bathroom. But she likes a long bath, and she hates people to disturb her when she's holed up in there. So I got myself a cheese and avo sandwich with loads of onion, seeing Trevor wasn't around to moan at the extravagance, and started making a few study notes on tidal pools. I was just coming to terms with sea anemones, when my mother yelled from the bathroom.

She just yelled my name.

"Da-a-vid!"

Now I'm used to my mother yelling my name, she does it all the time, but there was something in the way she yelled it that day that made me go cold. I rushed to the door.

"What, Ma? What is it?"

"Come . . . come here!"

I went into the bathroom. My mother was half-kneeling, half-crouching on the floor, naked, her wet hair plastered in ribbons around her shoulders, her eyes wide with terror.

"It's coming!" she said.

Another spasm gripped her, and it was true.

She stopped speaking altogether, although her mouth stayed open, and out of it came a long, deep moan. She hung on to the side of the bath, as though it was some kind of lifeboat and she was going under. As she moaned, she fixed her eyes on mine in a scary way, in a way that bore right through them, and out the other side of my head. It was as though she was looking at something else, as though I was no longer in the room. I almost turned around to check out what was behind me.

"O-o-o-o-o-O-H!" she moaned.

"Hold it, Ma! Just hold it right there! I'll get Trevor!"

A wave of panic pushed me out of the bathroom. Next thing I found myself at the telephone, the receiver clenched in my hand, listening to an engaged signal. Moan, moan, went the phone in one ear. Moan, moan, went my mother in the other. What the hell do I do now? I dialled again, to give the bastard a second chance – just like him to be unavailable in a crisis, my mother has terrible taste in men – but no, it was still engaged.

What now, what now! An ambulance? The Flying Squad? The police knew how to deliver babies, didn't they? The newspaper was full of cops who had babies named after them because they'd brought them safely into the world.

Taxi-drivers! Taxi-drivers had assisted the birth of millions on the way to the hospital!

Or Mrs Riviera, the owner of the toy shop four blocks away! She'd had five kids, she must've picked up something along the way!

Paralysed, I studied the pinboard which was stuck to the wall above the telephone, and noticed that the telephone account was three weeks overdue. Great! The telephone company was about to disconnect our service, then I wouldn't be able to get through to anyone at all!

I searched frantically around the living room for the telephone directory and eventually found it under a stack of old newspapers, then I remembered it was four years old. Do Flying Squad numbers change?

A headline caught my eye: "BREECH BABY DIES ON WAY TO HOSPITAL".

My heart stopped. I'd reckoned babies just flung themselves into the world like a ball out of a pinball machine at the beginning of a game. But things could go wrong. Things could go tilt, you could lose the game before you started. What if this baby was breech? What did breech mean? I rushed to my room and scanned the bookshelf for the dictionary, my very own, pocket money-acquired dictionary. It was missing.

Now, there were only two people who would've done such a thing without asking. Trevor and my mother. Don't ask me what for, because neither of them reads anything other than cereal packets and parking tickets. Which immediately made me suspicious, because, as I figured, if they aren't using my dictionary for literary purposes, they'd probably taken it to prop up the corner of the washing machine, or to light the braai.

That did it. I decided then and there that I wasn't going to be treated like a dog in my own house. I was going to stand up for myself, I was going to move out at the earliest opportunity and take an assertiveness training course.

"WHO TOOK MY DICTIONARY!" I yelled, storming through the house.

"Da-a-vid!"

That stopped me in my tracks.

My mother.

I swung a left into the bathroom. There she was, there they were, but for a moment I thought that I was on the wrong planet. Before me was a creature with two heads. "Help me!" said one of them.

It's hard to describe what happened to me at that precise point. I think it had something to do with being a Superman fanatic in my youth. I felt this calm descend on me, like Clark must feel every time he steps into a telephone booth. I could feel muscles bunching on my chest under my T-shirt, I could feel my jaw set. I went over to her and helped her down on to the bathroom mat.

"It's OK, Ma," I said, then looked at the baby's face, which was concertina'd around the top of its head, and was an alarming colour. Kinda puce, like left-over Youngberry Delight. Hang in there, baby, I thought. I'm gonna get you out of there, if it's the last thing I do.

"I wanna push!" screamed my mother. "Take its head, help me!"

I nodded, and took the baby's head gently between the palms of my hands. It was so small, so fragile, the wet wisps of jet-black hair plastered to the tiny skull.

Then I saw it. The cord. It was wrapped around the baby's neck.

Afterwards, I couldn't for the life of me remember how I'd known what it was I was seeing, nor that it was potentially a problem. Some ancient knowledge surfaced in my brain, as though my guardian angel took me on as her midwife apprentice and whispered a warning in my ear.

"Stop!" I yelled. "Don't push!"

And for the first time in her life, my mother actually listened to me. She lay there gasping and panting, while I slipped the loop of cord over the baby's head.

"OK," I said. "Now push, Ma. We've got to get it out of here!"

So she pushed, and the baby's head moved a little way further out. Then she stopped pushing, and the baby slipped back in, up to the chin.

I looked at my mother. "You have to push!" I urged.

She shook her head weakly, tears in her eyes.

"It's gone," she said. "The urge has gone." She must have seen the alarm on my face, for she added hastily, "It'll come back again. Just now. I told you these things take a long time!" She smiled at me, took my hand, and squeezed it.

"Thank you Davey. Oh! Oh, it's coming!"

I could almost see the wave passing through her body. I gripped the baby's head between my hands again and pulled, as gently as I could.

"You're doing great, Ma!" I encouraged her, although I was starting to panic again. What if this baby gets stuck? I thought. What if it's breech? What if they both die!

I began to pray, oh please God, help me, oh please, guide my hands, show me what to do! The flesh on the baby's face was so bunched up it couldn't open its eyes. I had to get it out now, or it would never open them.

Suddenly, desperately, I wanted to see those eyes open, staring at me.

"Push Ma! Forget everything else, just push!"

I couldn't get enough traction, I was sliding around on my knees in the blood and water on the bathroom floor, my hands weren't big enough, strong enough, gentle enough. If I didn't get this baby out, I would never forgive myself. "Come on, baby," I pleaded.

"Come on!"

And it did. It came right on, shot out of my mother's body like a miracle, and into the towel I'd laid on the ground; and then he, for I saw at once it was a boy, he opened his eyes and looked at me. His little brow wrinkled up with the effort of raising his eyelids, and as they slid away from the orbs of his eyes, I found myself falling, falling into the deep wells of his pupils. They just swallowed me up, enveloped me. He blinked and stared, blinked again. It was as though I could see the whole of creation caught up in that gaze, held, and reflected for my eyes only.

His little mouth opened, his face crumpled and with an ear-splitting wail, he began to breathe. He turned pink.

"The cord," my mother said. "We've got to tie the cord." She sat up and pulled a towel around her, her whole body shaking with the effort. "Get some string."

For once there was a ball of string in the kitchen drawer. My mother told me to tie the umbilical cord in two places and, with the meat knife, sever it between the ties.

"Call Sophie," said my mother. "Tell Sophie to come over and help."

Of course! Why hadn't I thought of that? Sophie was our next door neighbour. A doctor who worked night shifts. Why hadn't I thought of her?

Sophie helped my mother with the afterbirth while I put Kevin on the bed and cleaned him. I already thought of him as Kevin. He just looked like a Kevin. Once I'd washed all the white stuff off his skin, he started to look quite normal, except for the gross, waxy tube that stuck out of his belly. But he couldn't help that.

"You're a real beauty," I told him, so he wouldn't get a complex. "You'll see, you'll grow up to be almost as handsome as I am."

Seeing he didn't yet know about the devastating social set-back that comes with having chorbs, I thought he'd accept this pronouncement from me as fact. You can't start too early, I thought. After all, I'm his official brother. I'll have to give him some guidance in life. Rule number one: love your older brother and obey him, for he saved your life. It was clear, however, from the way he looked at me, that he was already my biggest fan.

Sophie checked him over and said he was fine. "You did well," she added. "Your mum told me about the cord around the neck."

I shrugged with embarrassment.

"Wrap him up, he mustn't get cold, and then let's feed him, he must be hungry." Sophie went through to the kitchen. "Your mum said there was a bottle in here, and some formula."

She wasn't going to breastfeed him. Why? Had she breastfed me? It'd never occurred to me to ask. I looked down at Kevin's little face. He deserved the best. Why wasn't she giving him the best? But when

Sophie brought the bottle and showed me how to feed the baby, I decided not to kick up a fuss. It felt so comforting to hold him, this tiny warm bundle nestling in the crook of my arm.

"Don't worry, Kevin," I reassured him. "We'll be all right. You'll see. We'll be all right."

Two

For about as long as I can remember I've wanted to be an explorer. I must've been about five when my grandmother took a book out of the library about adventurers and explorers and read it to me. Most of it went over my head, but the main idea stuck, going where no-one else had been, doing something no-one else had done, like climbing the highest mountain in the world, or racing to be the first to the South Pole.

I used to lie in bed and imagine that I was lying in a tent in the middle of the Amazon jungle with wolves howling outside, or snow-bound in Antarctica with polar bears sniffing at the tent flap.

Of course, at some point I learnt that there weren't any wolves in the Amazon, nor polar bears at the South Pole, and that people had lived for centuries in many of the places that famous people had claimed that they'd "discovered", like Livingstone and Da Gama in Africa, like Columbus in North America.

So I'd modified my requirement. It wasn't necessary for me to be the first person to do something, but the first person from my culture to explore something new to my culture. I mean, when Marco Polo explored Asia, he'd found an established culture that was more advanced than the one he'd come from in Europe. But imagine doing what he did, travelling all that way, by foot, on horseback, pushing his limits into the unknown, where at any moment the known world might give way forever, and you might be killed through ignorance, or a misunderstanding, or your own lack of judgement.

Or imagine being one of the first sea explorers, sailing off from Europe or Polynesia to the outer edge of the earth, where you could fall off into space, or be swallowed up by a sea monster. That took courage. The courage to trust in yourself, trust that the world wants to be explored, trust that we're not meant to languish in suburbia for the rest of our lives, with every whim on tap.

So from an early age, I set myself goals, projects that would test my endurance or strength or my limits on fear.

I would conquer the highest tree in the suburb, dive from the highest board at the public swimming pools, see how far I could swim underwater, go camping in the middle of the park all night, try to break the roller-skating record in the neighbourhood going down the hill near our house. That last attempt ended in disaster, for the only record I broke was for the number of bones broken in a roller-skating accident, both wrists and an elbow.

But that didn't stop me. Somehow, it seemed to me that a safe life wasn't a life at all.

On the other hand, dying wasn't for me either, not for a while yet, anyway. There were still too many mountains to climb, metaphorically speaking. Practically speaking, they'd all been climbed by other people. They went out and conquered the geographic North Pole. Then someone was first to reach the magnetic North Pole, then they invented a theoretical Point of Relative Inaccessibility, the point in the Arctic calculated to be the furthest in all directions from human habitation, and someone got there first too. People are running out of things to conquer all the time, so they start making up new ones.

Then there's the *Guinness Book of Records*. Eating two thousand bananas in ten seconds, or smoking a hundred and thirty cigarettes at the same time, that sort of thing, although I've heard they've stopped acknowledging gross records like that. Good for them. If you're going to die pushing limits, it might as well be while doing something that's theoretically healthy.

I thought at one point of becoming an astronaut, or a nuclear physicist, of getting off the surface of the world and exploring inner or outer space. People are still pushing boundaries there, at least until they meet the aliens coming the other way. Then they're back on chartered ground. But I think I've blown that one.

I was too busy exploring the Kalk Bay caves instead of studying maths to get good enough results in matric. And, except for the question on human reproduction, I pretty much messed up my biology paper. I just couldn't get my head into it, not after what I'd been through the day before.

So my other idea of becoming a doctor and being the first to find a cure for AIDS also bit the dust. Although I'm not exactly devastated by that. Looking down microscopes, and mixing things in test tubes and injecting innocent mice is a form of pushing the limit, I'm sure, but if you're stuck in a dingy lab while you're doing it, it's not for me.

No, I want to travel. I want to see the world. And that's just one of the reasons why everyone told me I was crazy to take on Kevin.

Three

Not that any of it was anticipated, or planned. I was just going to coochy-coo the little bundle until he was old enough to learn to play cricket. But the first thing that happened was my mother got into a serious depression.

She didn't want to feed him, or hold him, or even look at him much. It wasn't as though he was colicky or difficult. I mean, I hadn't even really noticed babies existed before Kevin popped out, but suddenly there were babies everywhere. Babies in prams on the pavement, screaming their heads off in shopping malls, getting in the way when we went roller-blading at the park.

Having noticed them, I reckoned I didn't really like kids, they didn't look like much fun. But there was something about Kevin that was special, that got through to me.

Maybe it had something to do with the birth, something in that first look that tied us in the same way a duckling attaches itself to the first thing that moves past it when it hatches, never mind if it's not its mother.

But my mother was blind to him. She couldn't see anything but the inside of her face, and she stayed in her room and cried and cried.

My stepfather got his old lady to move in to look after the baby and he went back to work.

"She'll get over it soon," was all he could offer.

I couldn't stand it. My step-gran was not my favourite person and she was openly irritated by my mother's state of collapse.

"I told you she's no good as a mother," she said pointedly to her son one suppertime. By the tone of her voice, and the way she didn't look at me, I knew that she was offering me up as an example of bad mothering. My hackles rose.

"She'll get over it," Trevor said lamely, forking food into his mouth. "She gets over everything eventually. You just have to weather the storm."

"That's the trouble with you," said his old lady. "You were always so passive. You always just lay there and let life pass you by. Now, you should go in there and give her a good talking to. She's got a baby to feed and look after. I'm not going to stay here and be her nursemaid forever."

"Mum, you don't understand. You don't know Tracey. You can't just 'talk her out of it'!"

"Well, you didn't seem to have a problem with talking me into coming here to look after Tracey's baby and Tracey! You're scared of her, that's what! Well, I'm not! I'm not going to do a song and dance routine around her! She's spoilt, if you ask me! She always gets her own way, manipulating everyone around her! It gets up my nose!"

"Then why don't you go home," I said coldly.

They both stared at me.

"Well I never!" said the old lady. "That's all the gratitude I get! Not even a thank you for this meal I've cooked, and he wants me to leave!"

"You aren't happy here," I said. "So it's better you go. I think your being here just makes everything worse."

She gaped at me in outrage.

"I can't believe what I'm hearing!" she said. "Now *I'm* the problem! I've sacrificed everything to come here and help out, and I'm told *I'm* the problem!"

She turned to Trevor. "Say something, you silly man! You must be at least partly to blame for this boy's upbringing!"

Trevor was looking at me strangely. "Yes," he said slowly. "I think David has a point. You aren't happy being here. Maybe it *is* best for you to go."

It took half an hour and the old lady was packed. Trevor took her to the airport. She didn't even look at me. When the front door closed on them, I felt relief wash over me.

Kevin started to cry, so I warmed a bottle of milk and picked him up.

"Well, little man," I said. "We've won our first battle. Let's drink to it."

And drink to it he did, his eyes fixed on mine as he grunted and panted and sucked until the bottle was empty and his little belly was as tight as a drum. Then I put him over my shoulder to wind him. That baby would win a burping competition any day. He'd make the regulars down at the Forrester's Arms look like rank amateurs.

"I'm really proud of you," I told him as I changed his nappy. "I reckon you'll go far." He looked at me with his deep dark eyes, aimed, and peed down the front of my shirt.

"I'll have to hire someone until your mother is well again," said Trevor worriedly. Money was always an issue in our household.

"No," I said. "I'll look after him."

Trevor sat back in his chair and looked at me.

"Oh, no," he said. "You've got to find a job. You've got to contribute to the income of this household. How long do you think you're going to sit on your bum and let me support you? It's been three weeks since you finished matric."

We'd had this conversation before.

The truth was I was feeling a bit depressed myself. My whole life loomed large ahead of me, and now that the dreadful routine of school was over, I had to decide how to live.

I knew what I wanted to do, but none of my ideas held the promise of bucks. And I had to make bucks. I couldn't stand being dependent on Trevor, particularly as he ground my face in it regularly.

What to do. Trevor said he could give me a job working at his garage, he would teach me, I could become a mechanic like himself if I worked my way up from the bottom. The thought of spending my life up to my elbows in grease, lying on my back, staring up at an internal combustion engine made me even more depressed, not to mention the thought of working for Trevor. I could tell he wasn't really enthusiastic about it either.

"No, thanks," I said. "I couldn't think of anything more boring." Which he, of course, took personally.

"The problem with you, young David, is you're afraid of a little hard work," he sulked. "You think that life is one long holiday."

I was sick of it. I told Rudd, my best buddy, about it. He'd fared even worse than I in the exams, except for English, and had to repeat matric. I felt sorry for him, but at least he didn't have to face the life crisis that I was in. He still had another year to think about what he wanted to do.

"Trouble is, there're no jobs. Even if there were any, you and me, we're the wrong colour. Only black blacks are employable nowadays."

Rudd put on his sunglasses and studied the burnt offerings strewn across the beach.

"The cosmic patterns are changing, the underdogs and the overdogs are changing place. You whiteys, there was a time when you couldn't go wrong. Now you're even the wrong colour for the hole in the ozone layer. But brown folk like me are stuck right in the middle, we don't go anywhere."

I loved Rudd's company. We balanced each other, we spoke the same language, read the same books. If he was feeling pessimistic, I would automatically feel good about things and it would rub off. And vice versa.

"Oh, I don't know," I said. "I don't intend to play this game by cosmic rules. I'm feeling lucky. I'm just going to follow my nose."

For that moment I did feel lucky.

"But, just to be on the safe side, slap some of this on to me, will you?" I handed him the bottle of suntan lotion.

"Well, at this present moment my nose is lined up with a certain member of the female species. So I'll follow it," said Rudd, brightening. "You stay here. I'll lead the advance party."

I watched him stride up to two girls who were sitting on the beach a little way off.

Rudd was not the shy sort, in fact, at times, I felt a little embarrassed for him. He didn't care if girls laughed at him, he didn't seem to get despondent when they dropped him after a couple of dates, if he got that far. It made me wonder what girls looked for in a man.

Rudd is just the greatest; he's funny, daring, and controversial. But he's not your stereotypical hunk and his chorbs are worse than mine. So in a way, I sort of admired him, venturing off like that, striking out alone across the beach to conquer two girls with boobs the size of Everest. No matter that he failed, and failed again, he never gave up. Surely that's what counted?

Surely one day his ship will come in, having sailed to the very edge of the known world? Surely some day a woman worthy of his great spirit would fall off the edge of the earth with him and they would float, suspended in the ether of love for the rest of their days.

My mother says I'm a romantic. She says that love is something stuck between a rock and a very hard place. She says that as soon as someone loves you for who you are, they set to work changing you into what they want you to be. Although I've not yet seen a man who's got very far with her.

Sometimes I get the impression that the men in her life are like planets circling around her fierce, raging self. Including me. It might even have been there on that beach that I decided I had to get away from her, break out of that helpless orbit. Maybe that's how the other guys in her life felt.

She and my father never speak to each other. They split up when I was only one year old, and I've only seen him a couple of times since then. I seemed not to exist for him, but it didn't really get to me. By the time I was conscious of his existence, I'd already latched on to my mother's next man as a father, so he filled the gap.

But then, when that relationship failed, and the next, I stopped getting involved with the men in my mother's life. I just gave them all up, including my father. I tried to regard them as part of the furniture, something that could arrive one day, and maybe leave the next.

I suppose sometimes I wondered about my dad. Whether he was a bum like most of the others. What'd happened to him. Last I'd heard, he was living up the coast in Knysna, making furniture. But that was some time back. I didn't even get birthday cards from him any more.

Down on the beach, Rudd seemed to be making some headway. One of the girls was laughing at him and letting him put suntan lotion on her back. He beckoned me to come over. Reluctantly I joined them.

"David, meet Yolanda and Rosemary. They tell me they've been ogling you ever since you set foot on Fourth Beach. It must be that sock you stuffed down the front of your costume."

This was typical. The girls shrieked with laughter, while I went several shades of maroon and promptly sat down in such a way that my groin was out of sight.

"I'll stuff a sock in your mouth," I warned him. But he was too far gone, too heady with success to heed any warning.

"David here, he's a black belt in karate, so be careful what you say to him," he warned Rosemary. "Be nice to him, or he might commit hara-kiri. Now I'm just going to the shop with Yolanda here to buy us all ice-creams. You two wait here."

Maybe that was it. Maybe he orchestrated everything too much, as though we were all actors in a great play where he was the director. I wondered how long he'd be able to hold it all together, how long it'd take before his plot broke down and we'd all go off in search of our own stories.

"Is he always such a jerk?" asked Rosemary. She

was of indeterminate age, as girls are between thirteen and twenty, and a bit too round in the face for my liking. But Rudd had been rejected for less, so I thought I'd give her a chance. Myself a chance for that matter, it was only through Rudd's bungling advances that I got into these situations.

Her question put me on the spot. I knew she would check me out by the way I answered. But the feeling passed. Rudd was my buddy. I wasn't going to use him as a cheap leg up.

"Actually," I said, "he's not really a jerk at all. He's great. He just acts that way around girls. I suppose it's an inverted display of shyness."

She smiled, her eyes straying. "You must go through an awful lot of socks in summer." She was trying to make me blush again, but this time I was ready.

"I see you have the same problem," I retorted, looking at her boobs, and was pleased to see her cheeks darken.

"Oh, no!" she protested, "They're real!" She looked at me angrily. "Look, what is it with you jerks? Leave us alone! Yolanda and I came down to the beach for a good time!" And she stood up, grabbed her and Yolanda's things, and stormed off.

Next thing, I see Rudd walking uncomfortably down the beach towards me. His hands were white and sticky from four ice-creams that were melting fast.

"What the hell did you do?" he demanded irritably. "One moment all was well, next thing Rosemary storms up, grabs one of the ice-creams, and rams it down the front of my costume! I'm probably sterile for life!" He sat down, and gave me two of the ice-creams.

"She couldn't take a joke," I said. "It wasn't my fault."

"After all that hard work," complained Rudd. "All for nothing."

"Well, we got two ice-creams each," I offered, trying to control the chocolate coating that was threatening to slide off into the sand.

Rudd glared at me. "Yeah, but I paid for them, remember?"

"I do," I said. "But I stopped them from being wasted on a lost cause. Those girls thought that we were jerks."

We ate on in silence. A thought struck me and I stopped eating.

"Say, Rudd, I don't suppose you remember which ice-cream she stuffed down your pants?"

Four

Which still left me in a predicament. How to earn an honest buck? I gave Rudd up as a lost cause when it came to discussing job opportunities and consulted Kevin. I was still his main care-giver while Trevor was at work, although my mother had emerged from her bedroom by then, emaciated, chain-smoking and withdrawn.

She did start doing some things around the baby, to the point that Trevor convinced himself that hiring someone wasn't strictly necessary, not until my mother went back to work after her maternity leave. But that particular day she was out, as she was increasingly while Trevor was at the garage, leaving me to mind the baby.

I was feeling really irritated. I mean it was *her* baby. I was starting to feel used.

I propped Kevin up in an armchair and went through the job section of the paper.

None of the jobs in there seemed like real jobs. Sales managers, bank clerks, research assistants. They all offered some weird notion of security – which was just a lure, behind which was the hungry cavernous mouth of the system, just waiting to gobble you up, to stick you in a box house with a TV and a family and a washing machine. I would rather die. There had to be another option.

Kevin squawked grumpily, arched his back and slid down the cushion. I sat down and crossed my right ankle over my left knee and propped him up in the triangle it formed.

"So what d'ya think, buddy?" I asked him.

It seemed to me, if he'd known how to speak, he would've been able to give an expert opinion on any topic under the sun. His eyes were the eyes of one who has travelled far, seen all manner of things. He surely had some idea about what I should do with my life.

"Let's start with my not inconsiderable talents, shall we?"

Kevin burped approvingly, and settled in.

"I am a great cooker of pasta. I can watch clouds for hours on end, and can fly a mean kite. I am not afraid of the dark or my own company. I am kind and generous, I play the guitar well. I love to read, and I can lift someone almost twice my own weight off the ground. I have become an expert at changing nappies without getting drenched, and I can dislodge the most stubborn of winds, both yours and mine."

Kevin regarded me steadily.

"So, what does that qualify me for? An au pair, at the very least. A Green politician, probably. But that leads me on to the next issue. It's entitled: 'The Things I Definitely Do Not Want To Be.' The list is endless, but amongst them are the following: a politician, Green or any other kind, an au pair, a teacher, a banker, a butcher, a TV soap opera star, an insurance salesman, a second-hand car salesman, a new car salesman, in fact anything to do with cars or selling, a lawyer, an estate agent, a computer programmer, a rubbish collector, a rubbish producer, a security guard, a mercenary, a soldier, a policeman . . . That sent you to sleep, did it? I don't blame you. There are millions of boring jobs in the world. And the thing is, if you do a boring job, you become a boring person.

"Now, if you'll let me continue, what I really want to do, is to be an explorer, only I don't know what kind yet and these things usually take bank loads of money. So, what's second best, huh? For the time being, until my real life starts. What'll get me as close to the excitement of exploring as possible without being able to do it?"

Kevin gave a large yawn and opened his eyes. Then he did it, for the first time in his short life. He smiled. He smiled at me. I was the recipient of his first expression of rapture, and what's more, he was only five weeks old at the time!

He's a genius, I thought, for I'd started on a couple of baby books that said babies only smile from six weeks of age. My brother is a genius. Like me!

I felt smiled upon by fortune, I felt blessed by evidence of someone else with brains in the family. Something was coming my way, I could feel it.

And come my way it did. It came in the form of an advert I wasn't looking for. I'd underestimated my buddy, Rudd. He phoned me up one day.

"I've got it!" he exclaimed.

"What, genital warts?"

"No, you moth-eaten windsock! I've got you a job."

My heart leapt and sank at the same time. Was this a hoax? Or some dead-end job tasting dog food? Again, I'd underestimated him.

"It says: 'Daring, yet sensible; physically fit and a good swimmer; a lover of nature and adventure; good with people; knowledge of first aid; aged between eighteen and twenty-four. If this is you, we want you!' I'd say that sounds like you."

"So get to the point! What is it?"

"Listen, you wax-eared pea-brain. Lucky for you, this ad doesn't ask about intelligence. You've got to apply by the end of this week to 'Adventure Rafters', and it gives the address. So? You interested?"

Of course I was interested! River rafting was one

of the things I'd never done because I was always broke. It had never occurred to me to be part of the operation!

"Rudd! You're a genius! I'm coming over now!"

Not that Trevor would consider it a real job. I didn't even know how much they paid or anything. All I knew was that my heart was singing. Here was a way out, a way in, whatever! And what's more, I'd be paid for having fun!

"Don't thank me," said Rudd. "I only did it to get you out of town so that you won't be around to stuff up my chances with the chicks."

I got the job. They liked the look of me and my enthusiasm must have all but knocked them out. Geoff, the manager of the outfit, was way cool. He explained that the work would take me out of town for up to a week at a time, which suited me.

I was sick of hanging around at home. Kevin's company was great up to a point, but the conversation was a bit one-sided. I did feel concerned about leaving him with my mother, who was not yet out of the woods.

"Go," she said, looking peeved. "Go out and have a good time, don't worry about me."

Trevor's reaction was predictable.

"Good God!" he said, putting his grease-stained

hands on his grease-stained hips. "I don't believe it! You really *do* think that life is a holiday! When *are* you going to grow up? How much is this outfit going to pay you?"

"It's none of your business," I said defensively. "I don't ever ask what you bring in!"

"Of course it's my business! You have to contribute part of your income to running this household. It costs me about one and a half thousand rand a month to house, feed and clothe you! Now that you're earning, that's what you'll have to hand over, minimum."

One and a half thousand rand! My starting salary was two and a half thousand rand a month, which had seemed like a fortune when they'd told me, but in the face of this information, it did seem a little paltry.

On the other hand, I suspected Trevor was pulling a fast one. I suspected he was trying to siphon money off me to subsidise his booze and cigarette addictions.

"Forget it," I said. "I'm going to be out of town half the month anyway. So that makes it seven hundred and fifty rand, maximum."

"All these years I've supported you and now you begrudge every cent that goes into helping this family survive! I've a good mind to put you out on the street, then you'll discover how tough it is!"

"Stop it!" shrieked my mother. "Stop fighting, you two! I can't stand this constant bickering. You're both driving me insane!"

She burst into tears, and so did Kevin.

I picked him up and patted his back. I was sorry he had to witness the stuff-up that was supposed to be family. I wished that I could take him away to a safe place, a place where there was laughter and hope and generosity.

I didn't want him to have the kind of life I'd had thus far, of moving house and changing fathers. Trevor wasn't going to last. I could see the signs already, my mother always out, the stony silences at meals, the screaming in the bedroom at night. And now Trevor was taking it out on me.

"It's the only way he'll grow up," he insisted. "He'll stay in this boy scout job for years and live here, getting me to subsidise his life, while he has a good time! He's got to realise that you can never be independent in that kind of job! Renting a place of his own would cost more than his whole salary!" He was in a real rage, pacing the room and red in the face.

"He's got to start somewhere!" objected my mother. "Give the boy a break! You're always so hard on him, so critical. It's a beginning, that's all!"

"I'm sick of this!" said Trevor, grabbing his jacket. "You two always gang up on me. You make me feel an outsider in my own family! I'm telling you," he said, pointing a finger at my mother, "until that boy leaves home, our relationship doesn't stand a chance. You've still got your umbilical cord wrapped so tightly around him that he can't even think for himself, he can't even begin to be a real adult in the real world!"

He stormed out of the house. We knew where he was going. To the pool tables, to the comfort of the bottle and the camaraderie of men.

His words stung me to the core. Did he ever stop to consider how much of a burden I'd taken off his shoulders by being around to help with Kevin and my mother? Ungrateful bastard. He couldn't even fold a nappy, he didn't even know how to massage my mother's shoulders when she had a tension headache. I stored these thoughts up for our next argument.

Five

White water dancing, brown power sliding past. The roar of the river as it shoulders past rocks, falling to the sea. There's something about rivers that mesmerises me, that holds me in its power. I could sense the river as if it were my own blood coursing through my veins. I learnt quickly that instead of fighting the water to stop my canoe capsizing, I could use the current to guide me and the movement of the water to balance me. Shooting a rapid was a dance, an exhilarating interplay of my life and body with the life and body of the river.

At night, when we stopped to camp on the banks, after Geoff or Dika or I had cooked for our clients and everyone had eaten and gone off to sleep, I would sit by myself for ages under the sweep of stars, watching the water slip by beneath a sheen of moonlight.

The calm after the rush of water and excitement was so soothing to me; it was a settling of myself, a long breathing out after the sharp breath in. The only thing that was missing was my guitar, but that, unfortunately, couldn't be helped.

"You should try it," I said to Rudd. We were sitting in his bedroom, listening to Salif Keita. We both had great taste in music. "It'll blow your mind."

"My mind blew already," he said. "I've met this chick, David. She's wilder than any rapid you care to mention. One day you'll grow up and realise that rivers are mere transitional objects that get replaced by the female of the species. Shooting rapids is a metaphor for the real-life experience of falling in love. I'm in the middle of a true suburban adventure. Her name is Cathy."

"Oh," I said, faking interest. "She got any sisters?"

Rudd shook his head slowly. "That's classified information until I'm certain this one's hooked. My groin has only just recovered."

"So . . . what's so great about Cathy?" I asked, trying to pick my words carefully.

At the mere mention of her name, Rudd all but disappeared into a stuporous soup.

"Everything," he said. "She's intelligent, funny, she can take a good joke. You know, that's really important. Never get involved with a stuk who can't take a good joke."

"I could agree with that," I said. "Good luck to you." My mind was already wandering, back to the outdoors, back to my life away from the cloistered maze of cement and metal, from the constant roar of traffic.

"You should try it," I suggested to Kevin, later on when I got back home. "In fact, I'll definitely take you one day. Let me know when you're ready."

"Awggggh," he said, for the moment more interested in trying to chew his way through a plastic rattle. He was developing so fast, it was amazing. Every time I came back home, I'd find him able to do something else, his face lit up with the pleasure of discovery. That's what a baby is, I thought to myself. An explorer of the first degree. To think we all did that, all babies explore the same things, their bodies, the world, their abilities, using all their senses, but for each one of them it's a brand new experience.

I wondered why most people stop exploring. Maybe it had something to do with school. At school you were told "facts" that other people had "discovered", and then you had to learn them. You never had to get into your own discovery mode. Babies, on the other hand, took nothing for granted, they questioned everything.

I watched Kevin, who was looking at his hand with astonishment, as though it had just arrived from another planet, and then cast my eyes down to my own hand. He was right. My hand was amazing, it was one

of the most miraculous things I'd ever seen; so intricate, so well-designed. So taken for granted.

A hand was not just a clever tool, it was a way into the soul, a map of fortune, a way we relate to each other, a means of giving and taking; love and gifts, punishment and violence. The whole of my body is represented here, in my hand, I thought. Possibly the whole of the universe.

I was so engrossed, I didn't notice that Kevin had crawled up to me. He grabbed my hand and pulled himself up on to his feet, using it as a support, then stood there wobbling on his unsteady legs and laughed at me, pushing his little forehead against mine, his dribble winding on to my leg. It was as though he was saying, lighten up a little! I laughed back at him, then took him in my arms and hugged him.

I couldn't understand why Ma didn't take more interest in him. She seemed irritable with him most of the time and got bored with him quickly. She'd gone back to work before the end of her maternity leave, saying she couldn't stand being at home any more, and a woman called Gladys came to look after him during the day.

At first I watched her suspiciously, wondering whether she was really up to the job. She seemed to spend a lot of time doing chores with Kevin wrapped up in a blanket or towel tied to her back. I was worried that he wouldn't get enough stimulation with his limbs strapped in, so he couldn't reach out for things, and not being able to see much besides her back. But he loved it and I realised that when he was with my mother he didn't get enough holding.

"Show me how to do that," I asked Gladys.

"What?"

"How to tie Kevin on to my back."

She burst out laughing, her lips stretching widely over her toothless gums. "Hayi, boetie," she chortled. "You haven't got the equipment."

"What do you mean!" I retorted indignantly, thinking that she was assuming that because I was a male, I didn't know how to care for a baby.

She beamed happily and wiped her hands on a dishcloth. "You haven't got any of these," she explained, cupping her massive breasts in her hands, "or any of these!" and she wedged her hands into her waist, her fingers spreading over her ample hips.

I saw what she meant. The blanket holding Kevin in place was itself held in place predominantly by these appendages. But I was determined to try. It didn't work. In order for the blanket to stay put on my pole-like body, Gladys had to tie the ends so tightly that it interfered with my breathing and digestive processes, and still Kevin began to slip after a few minutes. He announced loudly that he was fed up with the experiment, and only quietened down when he was transferred to the comfortable contours of Gladys.

"It's not fair!" I objected. "Nature is sexist! I want to be able to do that."

Not to be outdone, I spent some hard-earned money on buying a baby-carrier.

"We'll need it," I explained to Kevin. "We're going to do some exploring together, you and me."

He was only about nine months old when I started taking him up the mountain. It was good exercise too, he was loaded with puppy fat and jigged up and down in the carrier, gurgling with joy.

"Faster! Faster!" he seemed to be saying and I tried to oblige, galloping up Skeleton Gorge, or Lion's Head.

Rudd and I also took him to the public baths and, the two of us standing in the water a metre or two apart, we'd throw him to each other like a ball. He'd sometimes be submerged for a moment, before we pulled him out into the air, but he loved it, the thrill, the danger, the water.

"You're a child after my own heart," I told him. "I love you."

"I'll admit he's cute, as babies go," said Rudd, "but one day you'll grow up and realise your fixation with Kevin is just a diversion of your libido. Now that chick over there, she's the kind of babe *I'd* like to get involved with."

We were sitting on the grass next to the public pool, with Kevin trying to eat my big toe.

"What happened to what's-her-name, Cathy?"

Rudd shrugged. "She didn't have a sense of humour. Take my advice and never get involved with a woman who hasn't got a sense of humour."

I didn't comment, removed my toe and substituted a rusk.

"And she fell in love with someone else."

"That's a real shame," I said. "Keep your pecker up, one day you'll find a woman who sees the world down the same toilet as you do."

"What would you know about it," he retorted. "You know absolutely zip about love and even less about toilets."

That wasn't true. I had loved a girl once, in fact I still felt a pang whenever I saw her occasionally around town. Beverley had gone to the same school, but she'd been a year ahead of me and I knew that meant I was a non-starter. I'd once had a conversation with her at a party we'd both been invited to, but I'd been too terrified she'd reject me to even ask her to dance. There'd been a few girls who'd been interested in me, but, on the whole, I found girls younger than me boring.

That's a sweeping statement, and probably unfair, but that's just how it seemed. I just didn't like all the make-up and posturing, the interest in superficial things, like the shape of your nose and garage music. I hadn't met any that were interested in the things that fascinated me, like UFOs and Chick Corea and the Amazon.

The same went for men, for that matter. It seemed to me that the only kind of exploration that everyone of my generation was interested in was groin-related, from lipstick to fast cars. For me, the groin had to be connected to the brain somehow. Beverley, for example, turned out to be someone who wanted to be an archaeologist. I'll never forget that conversation we had at the party. It probably only lasted about half an hour, but in that brief space of time I found myself wishing I were a stone implement belonging to an ancient cave-dweller that Beverley could unearth and fondle.

I snapped back into focus to find Rudd striding out over the grass in one direction towards two hapless girls in microscopic bikinis, and Kevin striding out across the lawn, albeit on four limbs, in the opposite direction towards the deep end.

"It's a balance," I informed Kevin, hauling him back again, "between exploring life and staying alive."

"Ggggnnnaa!" protested Kevin, kicking his fat

little legs in an effort to free himself of this obstruction to his endeavours. I could see that as soon as I put him down, he would set off immediately for the pool again. I was right.

"No!" I said sternly, restraining him and wagging a finger. "No!"

"No!" said Kevin firmly, wagging his finger back at me. Again! A sign of genius! The child was only ten months old and already he was standing up for himself! "No!" he repeated, pleased as anything.

Rudd was beckoning, so again I plucked Kevin from his determined course and carried him, protesting all the way, over to where Rudd was sitting.

"Angie, Pippa, meet my friend, David. As you can see, he's already tied the knot, fully in love, unavailable and baby-bound. I warned him, but he wouldn't listen to me and now he's lost out on lovelies like the pair of you."

I half-laughed, half-groaned inwardly. Why did Rudd turn into a jerk at the mere sight of a woman? As it turned out, his attempt at stealing the limelight had backfired, for at once the two girls latched on to Kevin.

"Oh, he's lovely!" said one.

"How old is he?" asked the other.

Having a conversation while trying to stop a baby

from committing suicide is difficult at the best of times, so to make my life easier, I gave him back my big toe and instantly the world, for him, collapsed into digital proportions. He sat on the grass, chewing it contentedly.

"It's clean," I assured them. "I've just had a swim. Ow! Watch it, Kevin! You've got teeth now, remember!" He grinned wickedly at me and bit again. The girls were in hysterics. Rudd was in a sulk.

"That's the last time I take you to the public pool," he said later. "Why did you do that? You don't even like girls!"

"That's not true," I objected. "Although those two left me cold, I must admit."

"I must consider adopting a baby," he said. He looked at me sideways. "Do you think I can hire Kevin out on occasion? He'll bring the girls flocking like flies. I can always say that my wife died during childbirth. That'll get to them. Think of that."

Six

It was one of the happiest times of my life, working for Adventure Rafters. It made clear to me that life without adventure, without risk, is no life at all. And I could see on the faces of most of the people who came on the trips that they'd discovered this too. The only difference was that they came for one, or two, or four days, then they went back to their city jobs, whereas I, I worked on the river; the river and all that went with it was part of my life.

It was going home that I began to dread. I was always glad to see Kevin, he welcomed me warmly and cried inconsolably each time I left, but life with my mother and Trevor was increasingly horrendous. He was drinking more, she was out more, but on the occasions when they were in the same room, they needled and criticised each other until one of them snapped. It was so boring, so predictable. Sometimes the hostility in the room made it difficult to breathe.

"One thing's for sure," I told Kevin, who was sitting in his high chair. "I'm going to be very careful before I get involved with a woman."

"No!" he exclaimed fiercely, pointing a finger at me. We were now able to have conversations of a sort, although his vocabulary was monosyllabic and sometimes he didn't quite get the gist of what I was trying to say.

"Hot!" he warned. I thought he was giving me some sage advice about the nature of women, but then I realised that I was holding the kettle.

In the midst of the trauma at home, I was grateful that Gladys was around. She was easy-going and seemed genuinely fond of Kevin. I wondered what she thought about our disastrous domestic scene. My mother didn't seem to mind who was witness to her rages and Trevor was sometimes obviously drunk. But Gladys kept what she thought to herself, sticking to looking after Kevin and doing household chores. That helped my guilt at leaving Kevin, for I found myself staying away from home increasingly, even when I was back from the river.

Once I stayed at Rudd's place, who was gearing up for his matric exam once more.

"I can't wait to be rid of this drivel," he wailed, wrestling with a problem in geometry.

"Hang in there," I advised. "As soon as you've written your last exam, I'm going to take you canoeing down the Brede. I'll get you a discount trip. I'll even pay for it. I want you to come and experience it. It's not something I can explain."

"OK." He was really chuffed. He scratched his

dark, curly head, and pushed his glasses up his nose. "Help me with this first, will ya?"

"I couldn't," I said. "All that stuff fell right out of my head as soon as I'd written the exam. What are you going to do after matric, Rudd? You still planning to go into advertising?"

"I dunno. I'm thinking of taking a year off. Earn a bit of money. Try to connect with the things that matter to me again. This studying all the time has almost driven me out of my box. In fact, I've applied for a job as a barman at a hotel in Knysna for the Christmas holidays. It's where all the best chicks go."

Also where my dad had gone.

"Maybe you can look up my old man. Ask him if he remembers a guy called David."

"I could do that. It might be interesting to see where half your genes came from."

"He was a bastard, according to my mother."

I remembered a tall man with a beard. I remembered riding high on his shoulders. That was long ago. He could be a bum in the gutter by now. He could be a millionaire. It had nothing to do with me. I pulled my attention back to Rudd.

"You can't go until you've been canoeing with me, OK?"

"OK."

*

Things don't often work out as you've planned them. One Sunday evening I arrived home to find Trevor slumped in front of the TV, a beer bottle in his hand and a fag in the other. Tracey and Kevin weren't around. Trevor didn't even look up as I came in the front door, so I ignored him too, and went to my room. To my irritation, I found my bedroom door open. I marched into my room, and flung down my rucksack.

"Da!" said a happy voice behind me. I swung round. Kevin was sitting on the floor, surrounded by books he'd pulled out of the bookcase, which he was systematically destroying.

"NO!" I yelled in horror, lunging for him. His little face widened in astonishment, then crumpled, as I smacked his hand and yanked him off the floor. Immediately I felt sorry for him. It wasn't his fault! It was Trevor and my mother's! They knew not to open the door. Why did they anyway, invading my privacy! Incensed, I marched through to the living room, Kevin's wails accompanying me like a siren.

"What the hell were you and Ma doing in my room!" I demanded.

The slob turned towards me slowly, a grimace on his face.

"Why aren't you looking after Kevin? He's destroyed my books!"

Trevor stared at me, then looked back at the TV,

saying nothing, as though the full import of my words hadn't penetrated the alcoholic fog that surrounded his brain. I suddenly wanted to kick his stupid head in or shove it through the TV screen.

"I want full compensation!" I yelled. "There's hundreds of rands' worth of damage!" Money issues always got to him and my threat had some effect, for he swivelled his head slowly towards me again.

"She's gone," was all he said.

I didn't know what he was talking about. Then: it must be my mother. Gone where?

"What d'you mean?" Kevin was still shrieking away in my ear. "Oh, shut up!" I yelled at him, putting him down. "Where's she gone?" I demanded.

Trevor shrugged. "Don't know," he said. "Your bloody mother just buggered off. She left a note for you. In the kitchen, if you're interested."

It read: *My dear Davey, I can't take this any more. Please take care of Kevin. I'll be in touch soon. Love, Ma.*

"What happened!" I demanded. I stormed over to the TV and switched it off. "What the hell did you do to her? When did she leave? You bastard!"

Trevor burst out laughing. "That's a good one," he said. "What did *I* do to *her*? My dear boy, she's run off with the bloke you covered for all this time. And good riddance!"

"What on earth are you talking about?"

Trevor looked at me unsteadily. "Don't pretend you knew nothing! All those times you babysat, while I was at work supporting this family! You probably encouraged her, told her to go off and have a good time, hey? You always hated my guts, didn't you, for sleeping with your mother. Well, now, it's backfired on you, 'cause she's gone now and it's not only me she's left behind!"

"You're making this all up! How do you know she's gone off with someone?"

"She told me! She told me as she was walking out the door last night, all dramatic, tears pouring down her adulterous face. I should've known, that's what. I'm a stupid fool not to have seen it earlier, but she had you to cover for her, mummy's little boy!"

That did it. Something snapped, and I did something I'd never done before. I hit him, full in the face. It was the strangest feeling, my fist, tight and hard with anger, sinking into his soft face, the nub of his nose not giving way till the last moment, his face jerking back, the small but audible snap, the blood, pouring out of his nostrils. We looked at each other, astonished.

"Damn you," he yelled, groping for a hanky. "I should give you a good thrashing."

As it was, he drove us to the hospital. When I'd

reached down to pick up Kevin, I'd felt an excruciating pain shoot through my right hand.

"It'll serve you right if it's broken," said Trevor. "You're the same as your mother. Blaming your problems on me."

For a moment I was tempted to hit him again, with my left hand to finish him off once and for all, but he was driving and drunk into the bargain.

I looked out of the car window into the night, at the city of lights and wondered where my mother was. She'd come back. She'd never leave me behind. Nor Kevin. It was Trevor she was trying to get away from. She'd be back.

The gods were on my side. My hand wasn't broken, but Trevor's nose was. My hand was sprained and the doctor told me to rest it for a week or two, so I couldn't go back to my river, nor play my guitar.

I was terrified of being stuck at home with Trevor, who was also off work for a while after his nose job, so I got Geoff to let me work in the Adventure Rafters office while I healed.

First thing Monday morning, I phoned my mother's work. Her boss sounded surprised by my enquiry and told me she'd taken her annual leave. As I put the phone down, a coldness crept over me. What if she *had* left? What would become of Kevin and me? I rang Cheryl, her friend.

"D'you know where Tracey is?" I asked her. She claimed she didn't know any details, only that my mother was unhappy and had talked about leaving Trevor repeatedly. I had to ask her about the other thing.

"Did she tell you about another man?"

"Ye-es. She told me that she'd met someone else."

"Who?" I demanded. "What's his name?"

"Simon. That's all she told me."

"Listen, Cheryl, if my ma contacts you, you must get her to phone me. Or find out where she is. There's a toddler here who needs his mother. OK?"

"OK," she promised. "And David," she said, "let me know if there's anything I can do."

"That's all you can do. Just help me find my ma."

Seven

"She'll be back soon," I assured Kevin. Changing the nappy of a wriggly one-year-old with a left hand and an elbow is more of a challenge than climbing a rock face.

"Lie still, Kev! There must be a better system than nappies. I'm going to invent one. A wet/dry vacuum cleaner on wheels that's attached to waterproof pants. It just sucks everything up. And it would stop you from crawling around and getting into trouble. Kevin, your brother is a genius!"

I was trying to keep his mind off his mother. Our mother. I just couldn't stand the thought that I couldn't get hold of her, that I still didn't know where she was.

"Maybe she's in trouble!" I said to Trevor. "Maybe she hasn't gone off with someone else. Maybe she's driven over a cliff! Did you think of that?"

He paused for a moment in the middle of his breakfast and contemplated me quizzically.

"Well, I don't know about you," he said. "But if I was about to commit suicide, I wouldn't bother to pack my clothes and my toothbrush and empty my husband's bank account. But maybe you have a point. I mean, the Egyptians believed you could take material wealth with you into the next world. If so, she's very well equipped." He turned back to his egg.

I hated him. He didn't care about my mother; no wonder she'd left him. But what he'd said was true. The first bit. I'd gone through my room and found that a photo of me had gone. That was probably why she'd been into my room. To think that's all she had of me, a photo. She'd said that she'd be in touch soon, but what was soon? My mother wasn't famous for keeping her word. "Soon" could be next year, or the year after, if she was having a good time. But if she was miserable, then chances were she'd phone next week. I hated her too.

Sure enough, the next evening the phone rang. I rushed to it, as I had every time it rang. I didn't want Trevor to get there first, in case it was my mother and they had a row and she put the phone down.

"Hallo, Davey."

"Ma! Where are you?"

"Oh, Davey, I'm having a terrible time! Simon's broke and so am I. I don't suppose you have a bit of money to lend me? I'll pay it back at the end of the month, I promise."

I was stunned. My mother could be callous, insensitive, selfish, but this took the biscuit.

"I don't know how you could do this!" I said. "How could you just leave us?"

"What d'you mean?" She sounded truly astonished. "You're the one who left, when you took that lousy job! You're never at home! I didn't even think you'd notice I was gone!"

"I've got to work, Ma! And what about Kevin? He needs you!"

"He's got a father too! You think I'm going to sit around at home while that drunk is out, putting his hands all over some other woman! Let him do the baby bit for a while! I'm up to here with your father!"

"He's not my father!"

"No, you're right, but he's made of the same stuff!"

I could feel rage pushing up from way, way down. "And the guy you've got now? What stuff is he made of, huh?"

"He's a good man, Davey. He treats me well."

"That's what you said about Trevor, Ma! And you call *me* a romantic!"

"Listen, I don't have to stay on this phone and listen to this abuse! I just phoned to see if you were OK, that's all!"

"Ma, where are you? No, don't put the phone down!" It was too late.

The line buzzed in my ear.

*

"I'm putting him up for foster care."

We were eating supper together, which was an unusual event, nowadays. Kevin was in his high chair, insisting on feeding himself, so his face was awash with a blend of mashed banana and the remains of a cold. At first I didn't understand. Then Trevor's words sunk into my brain like a pitchfork.

"What?" I stared at him in amazement, then looked at Kevin. Thank God he doesn't understand, I thought. "Are you out of your mind?"

Trevor looked at me defensively. "No," he said. "But it seems to me that you haven't used yours."

Trevor was good at this. This was the one thing that he was really good at. You better watch it, I thought. Your nose has only just healed.

"Look at him," said Trevor. "Just look at him." We looked at Kevin, who was trying to feed the cat his mashed banana. "He's not mine. He doesn't look like me, not one bit."

It wasn't true. He couldn't tell. It was true that Kevin was about ten million times more good-looking than Trevor, but he had the same sort of mouth. Sort of.

"How dare you!" I said. "You've got a bloody nerve!"

Trevor folded his arms across his broad chest. "Either you're very naïve, or you're a good actor."

"It's you who's been cheating! If Ma's run off with

someone else it's because you have a girlfriend! She told me! And this mess has got nothing to do with Kevin! Don't you try to bring him into this! Anyway, I wish it were true! I wish Kevin wasn't your son! You don't deserve him!"

Trevor sat unflinchingly in his chair as I dropped this avalanche on him. He doesn't care what I say to him, I thought. He really doesn't care.

"You know, David," he said slowly. "For once you might be right. Neither Tracey nor I deserve Kevin. That's why I want to put him up for foster care. When your mother left she took her contribution to the household expenses, and she took with her what this child needs to grow up in the world. He needs a mother. I can't be his mother. And now I can't afford Gladys."

He set the beer down on the table and studied it. He didn't look at me as he said this, just talked to the beer bottle, as though it alone would understand.

"Face it, David, your mother is a stuff-up and I have some problems too. Kevin would be better off somewhere else, at least for the time being."

I was too stunned to answer just yet. I just stared at this excuse for a person and wished with all my might that my mother had never met him.

"If your mother comes back, if she straightens herself out, maybe we can talk about it, maybe I can forgive her, maybe I can accept Kevin as my own and bring him home again. But with things as they are . . . it's better he's fostered." He shook his head and drained the bottle.

A coldness settled over me. I knew what was going on. I felt it in my bones, an ancient knowledge. Trevor was using Kevin to get at my mother. I looked at Kev, oblivious to what his father was saying, busy turning his supper into an art work, banana in his hair, and I knew that I wasn't going to let them. I'd had no-one to defend me at that age. But Kevin had me.

"No," I managed to say, through the pressure of tears. "You can't give family away. I'll take him."

Trevor shot me a sharp glance. "Don't be ridiculous," he said.

"It's you who's ridiculous! Even thinking of giving away your own son!"

"You're so young," he said angrily, "so naïve. Do you think I wanted things to turn out like this? Well, what's done is done, you still have to learn how hard life is."

I was so sick of his attitude, so tired of hearing his voice, thin with self-pity.

"*You* make it hard! You pretend it can't be any other way! Well, it's going to be different for Kev and me! I'm grateful to you for showing me one thing in all the miserable time I've spent in your company.

That I'm not going to be like you! And neither is Kevin!"

Trevor stared at me. For one moment I thought I'd gone too far. Then, with what felt like a slap in the face, he started to laugh mirthlessly.

"Oh, yeah," he said. "And what do you plan to do? You can't even support yourself, let alone take care of a baby."

I stood up, grabbed Kevin out of his high chair and slotted him on to my hip.

"I'll think of something. If it's the last thing I do, I'll think of something." I had to. It was a matter of life and death and not only for Kevin.

There was no way I was going to live with this drunken mechanic for the rest of my life.

Eight

One of the most important things an explorer has to cultivate is a good relationship with his or her guardian angel. Not only because you need someone to snatch you up in the nick of time from the lunge of an avalanche, or just before you slip over the edge of a waterfall. You also need company. When you're out there on your own in the wilderness, or even in those moments before you fall asleep, you need someone to sound things out with, to pour your heart out to.

The first time I became aware of my guardian angel was when my gran read a book to me about them. The book said that guardian angels always looked after you and protected you from danger.

"But Gran," I asked her. "Then why do bad things happen in the world?"

She had to think about it a bit. "Well, Davey, the more you get to know your guardian angel, the better she can protect you. But even then, bad things can still happen to you. Your guardian angel is there to help you get over what happened."

And I found what she said to be true. Whenever I

felt sad or afraid, I would ask my guardian angel for help. Especially after my gran died and I had to go back to living with my mother. I would lie in my bed at night, trying not to cry and my angel would come and stand at the bottom of my bed. I knew it was my angel, because she had my gran's face. But as I grew older, my guardian angel changed and started to look like Superman. I knew that I could call on him at any time and he would be there to help me. I could be standing in line, waiting for assembly and the teacher might have shouted at me for not having the right socks on. Meanwhile my mother hadn't got around to buying the right socks and I would just think of him, standing behind me, with his cape around my shoulders and the power of that feeling would stop my tears before they started.

That night, when I put Kevin to sleep, I thought it was time to tell him about his guardian angel. It looked as though he was going to need one.

"Kev," I said, lying down on my bed next to him. "There's something that you need to know."

"Ummma," he said.

"You've got a helper that you can call on any time of the day or night."

"Tinkle, tinkle, sta!"

"Yes, kinda like the twinkle star. I'm also here to help you, Kev, but if anything should happen, you must remember your angel star."

He looked at me with his deep blue eyes and I had the feeling that he understood.

As for myself, I hadn't considered my guardian angel for some time. Not for years, in fact. As I lay in bed that night, I could feel my fear and loneliness, clammy like the darkness around me, my anger like a burn in my gut. Where the hell was Tracey? Surely she knew what a bastard Trevor was by now? It wasn't true that she expected Trevor to "do the baby bit" for a while, she knew I'd take over where she'd left off. In fact, she'd asked me to do just that! I was tired of her doing one thing and saying another. It was true what Trevor's mother had said, much as I hated to admit it. Ma manipulated us all.

Alone. It was different from the kind that I looked for and found beside a river or up a mountain, the kind that made me feel at one with nature. It was like being trapped in a deep cold pit, one that made me so small and helpless I could die. The only person in my life who'd given me help, unasked and unconditional, was my gran. She'd brought comfort and happiness to my early childhood, she'd filled the gap when there was no-one, only pain. But she was dead, I couldn't reach her. And the gift she'd given me?

My guardian angel.

I looked at the foot of my bed, but there was only an ugly veneer cupboard. I closed my eyes, to see whether I could sense a presence, but there was only the feeling of dread crawling along my skin like snails. Then I really started to panic. I had lost touch with something central, something important, the only thing that could see me through.

I lay into the night, conjuring up memories of my gran, pitifully few, for she'd died when I was only seven; I lay tossing and turning, unable to sleep.

At last, hot and maddened, I got up and went to have a shower. And standing there in the pelting cool burst, it came to me. Go to Knysna. Kev and me, we'd go with Rudd to Knysna. In an instant, I felt my skin relax. That hadn't been my voice.

That was my guardian angel speaking.

I dried myself off, went to bed and slept like a baby.

"You're stark raving mad," Rudd said. "Fortunately, that's a quality I admire." He had finished writing his exams and we were celebrating in a noisy, smoky pub.

"So?" I asked, "Is it on? Can we come with you?"

He eyed me slowly. "You sure this is the right thing to do?"

"Why, can you think of anything better?"

"You could run away and join a circus. I can see the banners already: "'Come and see the amazing Driver brothers! Living proof that dysfunctional family life produces morons!'"

"Rudd! For god's sake, this is serious! What on earth am I supposed to do?"

"I dunno. But this is one hell of an option. Look at you, you're young, virile and almost as handsome as I am. For the first time you have a life, a job. You gonna give that all up? I've got younger brothers, I know about these things. Full-time isn't easy. So far all you've done is change a couple of nappies. You gotta consider this one carefully, man."

I felt irritated with him, cornered. I'd be giving up my river. I felt sick to the heart.

"And now your ma throws you a hot potato," continued Rudd. "In my opinion, you should throw it back. Holding on to it, you'll just get scalded." He looked pleased with his metaphor.

"I can't, Rudd, damn it! She's disappeared."

"Get the police to find her. Put her picture in the paper."

I was ashamed enough of my family without doing that. I shook my head. "Look, Rudd, I'm leaving town with Kevin. I don't see another way out. If you want company, let me know. If not, I'll find someplace else to go."

Although it was Knysna I'd set my heart on, I wasn't yet ready to let on to Rudd why. Or even myself, for that matter.

"Don't get me wrong! You're welcome to come

with me. As long as you understand I'll be earning a pittance. You got any bucks?"

"Yeah, I've been saving. And I'll get a job there."

"Goodbye, Adventure Rafters."

"There'll be other adventures," I said determinedly. "I'm sure Knysna's full of them."

"Babies and adventures don't go together," warned Rudd.

I shot him a sharp look. Who did he think he was?

"This baby's not going to change my life," I said. "It's just a question of attitude. He'll fit in."

"I hate to point this out to you, buddy, but he's already changed your life. And if it's adventure that you're after, I would've thought that kidnapping a baby is enough adventure for a lifetime!"

"I'm not kidnapping Kevin!" I was shocked. "He's my brother! And Trevor's only too glad to be rid of him."

Rudd looked at me. "I hope you're right," he said.

I hadn't thought of it that way. But it was true. Trevor, or even my mother, might see it in that light and kick up a fuss. I didn't want to ask Trevor in case he said no. And I couldn't check it out with Tracey. Anyway, she'd asked me to look after Kevin. And Trevor was a drunk. Anyone could see that he was unfit to be a father. He wanted to give his own child away! Let them take me to court, I thought. Let them try to get Kevin away from me! I'd fight them to my last cent! It'd be a very short fight, but I was determined to win.

"When do we leave?" I asked.

Rudd smiled. "I only have to report for duty in a week's time. But I'm ready when you are. We could leave right now, if you want."

I studied his face. He wasn't joking. "OK," I said. "Let's go."

Trevor was asleep by the time I got home, so it was easy. I threw Kevin's and my things into a suitcase and a rucksack and packed them, my tent, two sleeping bags and my guitar into Rudd's car. Then I carried the sleeping Kevin out of the house and got into the back seat with him. A tiny stab of guilt poked me back into the house, where I left a note for Trevor, saying I'd phone him.

Then we were off, heading down the highway into the night. I love travelling at night. It's like flying through space. I began to feel much better. Something else would happen now, I felt sure, something good for a change. I've escaped, we've escaped. No-one can touch us. We're the three best people in the world, setting off into the unknown.

Somewhere around Riversdale, Kevin woke up. He sat up in astonishment and looked out of the window.

"Sta!" he said, pointing a crooked, sleepy finger. I gave him a hug.

"Yes, Kevin. We're going exploring. We might even reach the stars if Rudd's jalopy picks up a bit more speed."

"Are you complaining?"

"Nope! No-one's complaining around here, are we, Kev?"

"Dummy!" complained Kevin. Dummy. I'd forgotten the dummy.

"Stop!" I said to Rudd. "We've got to go back!"

"What! What for?"

"Kevin's dummy. I forgot it. He's hooked, he'll have withdrawal symptoms, he'll be up all night, every night if he doesn't have it. Believe me, life will be unbearable."

"Nonsense," said Rudd. "He's old enough to transfer his oral hang-ups on to the bottle. Or cigarettes."

"I'm serious, Rudd! He's got to have it! We've got to turn back!"

"Dummy!" wailed Kevin.

"I'm not turning back for any dummy! We'll get him another in Knysna. There must be dummies in Knysna. Give him your thumb to suck meanwhile."

I tried this, but Kevin spat it out in disgust. "Dummy!" he implored. "Dummy! Dummy! Dummy!"

"I knew we should have brought a chick with nice boobs along with us," said Rudd. "Hang in there, Kevin. There'll be plenty in Knysna."

But Kevin was inconsolable. He wailed and sobbed, until I couldn't stand it any more. I knew how he felt. He'd lost his ma and his pa; now he'd lost his dummy too. I grabbed my guitar, which was stashed in the back.

"Listen to this, Kev," I offered and started up a blues riff. "Here's another piece of advice to you, direct from your older, more experienced brother. When you're down, sing the blues. Like this:

"I've got the deep down blues,
The left-town blues,
The high-wailing, down-tailing, deep-frown
    blues.
And if you ask me why
I'm startin' to cry,
It's 'cause my dummy and me, we had to say
    goodbye.

"You got it Kev?

"I've got the pit-stop blues,
The hip-hop blues,
The mean-talking, slow-walking, flip-flop blues.

'Cause I went out of the door,
Don't have dummy no more,
Now my eyes are red and my heart is sore."

Kevin had stopped crying and was sitting mesmerised. He loved it when I played to him and I would often make up a song as I went along.

"That's good!" laughed Rudd. "That's really good! More!"

"More!" agreed Kevin, clapping his hands.

"I've got the no-hope blues,
The hang-rope blues,
The nose-running, hip-gunning, tele-soap blues.
'Cause my baby and me,
Forgot the dummy,
The CD player, the whisky and the bloody
    TV!"

The dawn was breaking by the time we reached Knysna, what with a flat tyre on the way. But we were all in good spirits, having sung ourselves hoarse for most of the way. We got some grub at a café that was just opening, then pitched my tent at a camp-site near the lagoon. We were wrecked. Rudd and I zipped up the flap to prevent Kevin from wandering and got into our sleeping bags. But Kevin thought that it was still party-time and sang "Tinkle Tinkle Sta!" loudly enough to wake the police.

"Kevin," said Rudd sternly. "That's a lullaby. You must sing it softly."

Kevin thought it was a big joke and sang even louder, trying to sit on our heads and poking biscuits into our ears.

After a while, Rudd sat up. "We're going home," he said. "Or *we're* putting him up for adoption. I can't stand this any more."

"Lie down," I advised him. "Ignore him completely. If you respond in any way, he takes it as a sign of encouragement. You'll see, if you pretend to be asleep, he'll join us soon."

Which he did and we all slept soundly until around lunch-time, when the owner of the camp-site woke us to demand payment. I could see by the way he looked at Rudd that he didn't feel comfortable with black campers. He's going to give us a hard time, I thought. But Rudd, as always, rose to the occasion.

"Vell," said Rudd in a dreadful German accent. "I haff neffer been zo batly treated in all my lyff! Ve iss tourissten commin to zee your country, unt ziss iss how you spick to uss!"

I struggled to keep a straight face, but, incredibly, it worked! The old geezer offered us the best site

overlooking the lagoon and said that we shouldn't
bother to pay until we left.

"Right," said Rudd when the owner'd split.
"Let's hit the beach."

Nine

Another important thing about exploring: Don't panic.

Of course, this is a constant possibility when you're striking out into the unknown. You may have some very good ideas about where you're going, or even what you've set out to do, but they're only ideas. When you get there everything is likely to look very different. You might not recognise anything at all. That's when you think you're lost. And you panic.

Well, sitting on that beach in the sun's embrace, the edge of the wide lagoon shushing coolly up to my feet, watching Kevin fervently immersing himself in the experience of sand and water, I panicked.

What am I doing here? I thought. Right now the police are on my tail, Adventure Rafters will sue me for breach of contract, we'll starve, Kevin will be taken away from me for good, Trevor's right, I'm not fit to parent him, my life's only beginning, I'm too young for this. I must be out of my mind.

I phoned Trevor from a nearby tickey-box.

"Where the hell are you?"

What to tell him? I couldn't trust him with the

truth. But he would find out one way or another. He just had to discover that Rudd had left town on the same day. Better to play this cool.

"We're in Knysna. Don't worry, Trevor. Kevin is having a great time. I'm going to get a job here, settle down maybe."

There was a snort on the end of the line, I couldn't tell whether it was of disgust, disbelief or anger.

"How's your nose?" I asked with as much concern as I could muster.

"You're crazy," he said. "I've got a good mind to let you find out the realities of life the hard way, but it wouldn't be fair on Kevin."

"Since when are you so concerned about Kevin? And why do you always put me down! I was fine as a child-minder all this time when you and Ma wanted time out, but suddenly I'm no good any more!"

"You're a dreamer, David. You're too sentimental. And you're irresponsible. You had no right to run off without discussing this with me first!"

"Look, you got what you wanted. You've got Kev and me off your hands. You're a free agent. Your girlfriend can even move in without embarrassment now."

"Cut the bullshit, David! I don't have a girlfriend! Your mother's not going to like this, I'm telling you!"

"Ma asked me to look after Kev!"

"Somehow I don't think she had it in mind for you to run away with him!"

"If she's unhappy about it, she can come and get him."

"Oh, it's only what your mother thinks that counts!"

"Look, Trevor. You don't want Kevin right now. I do. Just give us this chance."

There was a silence for a while on the other end of the phone. Then, when Trevor spoke again, I thought I heard a seam of sadness in his voice.

"If that baby gets harmed in any way, David, I'll make you pay for it."

"I love him, Trevor. He's in good hands." What I really wanted to say was: It's you who's harmed him, I'm the one who's saving him! But seeing that I was making some headway, it wouldn't have been wise.

"And, David?"

"Yeah?"

"Phone me. Every couple of days. Let me know how he is, what's going on."

What a drag. But part of me felt sorry for Trevor. He was all alone, in that tasteless, middle-class suburban house. He'd lost everything.

I phoned Adventure Rafters next and filled in

Geoff. Predictably, he wasn't wild about my change of plans, but he was buddy enough not to kick up a fuss. I'd told him about Kevin and he probably understood, having a kid of his own. He even said that if I came back to town and there was a position going I should reapply. So it was with considerable relief that I hung up the receiver. Two difficult phone calls and they had both gone my way! I must be doing something right.

Back at the camp-site, Rudd had made a fire and had some sausages on the go.

"Where's Kevin?" I said, panic gripping my throat. I hadn't been certain about leaving Kev with Rudd while I went to the phone, but he had given me his word he wouldn't let him out of his sight. But now the baby was nowhere to be seen.

"In there," said Rudd, pointing to the zipped-up tent. "He kept on wandering off and then he did something unforgivable."

"What?" I said, opening the flap and upon doing this, the answer became self-evident.

"You've got to potty train him," said Rudd. "You have to teach him sociable behaviour."

"At this point," I said, hauling a clean nappy out and trying to persuade Kevin to lie down on his back, "I have to remind you that not so long ago you were doing the very same thing."

"Yes," said Rudd, wrinkling his nose, "But I didn't have to clean it up."

"Keep your complexes about your bodily functions to yourself," I advised him. "This is all part of growing up, hey, Kev?"

There was also the issue of washing the nappies. I would have to do them by hand as a launderette gets expensive.

"Fortunately it's summer, so you can go bare bum most of the time," I pointed out to Kevin. "But I'm going to have to get a job soon. And that means crèche for you."

"I start this bar job in a week's time," said Rudd. "Come to the hotel tomorrow. Maybe they can fix you up with something, too."

I didn't exactly fancy serving people drinks for a living, but it was better than nothing while I looked around for something else.

I went along with Rudd the next day. The manageress said they had no vacancies at the bar. "The only job we have going is musician," she said. "The guy we hired let us down at the last moment."

"Well, you're in luck!" exclaimed Rudd. "This friend of mine is totally useless at serving anything, even a tennis ball, but when it comes to music, he's a natural!"

The manageress looked at me doubtfully. "Well, let's hear you," she said.

I couldn't believe my ears. This would be great, but could I do it? Most of the stuff I liked to play wasn't exactly commercial enough for pub life. And I had never performed in public before. But I got my guitar out of the car and tuned up.

I played a couple of songs from Clapton's 'Unplugged' as the manageress looked about Tracey's age. Turned out that the manageress was a Clapton fan and that was it. I was hired. I gave Kevin a hug as we left the hotel.

"We're going to have to practise in the next week, mate. Perhaps you can do the chorus line."

After his initial excitement at having got me a job, Rudd slid into a slump.

"I don't believe it," he groaned. "I've gone and shot myself in the foot again."

"How's that?" I asked.

He glared at me. "Y'know, I came here to earn a bit of money and score with the chicks. And what do I do? Out of misguided motives I bring you along and you end up with a glamorous, high-profile job, centre-stage, right in the same room as I'll be working. There's nothing more sexy to females than a long-haired, guitar-wielding crooning male. I may as well leave town!"

I put my arm around him.

"Never mind, Rudd," I said. "I'll be your front

man. I'll get their attention, then I'll tell them you taught me how to play the guitar and I'll pass them on. Promise. I'll tell them I'm unavailable."

Rudd groaned still loader. "You don't get it!" he wailed. "You still don't get it! The next most attractive thing to chicks is a man who says he's unavailable!"

"We'll see. I bet you find a girlfriend first. But don't try so hard. When you're out there, exploring the volcanic ground of sexual relationships, you've got to tread lightly, or you'll set something off that you didn't expect."

I don't think that Rudd was listening to this sage piece of advice. Come to think of it, neither was I.

Ten

I met Jill in the children's section of the library the following day.

I'd decided to introduce Kevin to the idea that books were not just objects to be shredded. We were just settling down to a story about a puppy let loose in a supermarket, when a woman about my age sat down on a stool opposite us.

She was very striking, not because she was beautiful in any conventional sense, but because her face was strong and full, almost defiant. Her blue eyes were accentuated by heavy eyebrows and her dark hair fell to an abrupt line just below her shoulders. She had a child with her, a girl, slightly older than Kevin, cheeks so round that they hid the bone structure of her face.

She started young, I thought, then realised I could be wrong. People were always making incorrect assumptions about my relationship to Kevin. Maybe she was the child-minder, or a sister.

"Excuse me," I began. She looked over at me in a slightly irritated way. "I . . . um . . . well, I just wondered whether you knew of any child-minders in this town? For my child?"

I indicated Kevin, then realised what I'd said. I was saying it more and more often. I thought of him as my child. He should've been my child. Kev couldn't help it that the stork had such lousy navigational abilities.

"Well, I . . ." but she was interrupted by an ear-splitting shriek. We swung around to see that Kevin had made a grab for the little girl's lollipop. She'd retaliated by bashing him over the head. By the time we'd separated them, they were both in tears.

"They're worse than dogs," I said. The woman frowned at me for a moment, then gave a short laugh.

"Well, they're more honest than adults," she retorted. "They let you know exactly how they feel." She had a point. If I'd had the honesty of Kevin, I would have grabbed her. But then, she'd probably bash *me* over the head.

"They also have less insight. I mean, Kevin should've known he'd get clobbered."

She smiled, her eyes steady on mine. "He'll learn." She turned her attention to the little girl, who was still wailing. Kevin had given up on women and had started to unpack the bookshelves.

"Excuse me." The librarian towered over us. "Eating is not allowed in the library."

I quickly checked to see whether Kevin was

sampling any books, then realised she was referring to the little girl's lollipop.

"C'mon, Tamsyn." The woman stood up and grabbed the child's hand. "Let's go."

I'd blown it! And without Rudd's help! I sat looking after her as she marched out of the library. Then the adventurer, the one who never gives up, took over. I wasn't going to leave it at that. "C'mon, Kevin," I urged. "Let's go get lollipop."

We charged out of the library after her. The woman walked swiftly down the main road, unaware she was being followed, although Tamsyn, who was slotted on to her hip, kept us under surveillance over her shoulder, pulling faces at us. Kevin thought this was as good as a car chase in a movie and gurgled me on enthusiastically.

Rudd would be proud of us, I thought. I wish he were here to see this.

At the other end of town, the woman swung into a shop. I slowed down, then entered at my leisure. It was a pottery shop, with displays in the window and on racks around the walls. At the back of the shop was a workbench and a pottery wheel. A woman dressed in overalls and an apron was working the wheel, between her hands a lump of clay was changing shape, as if by magic. I watched, mesmerised. The woman with the baby was nowhere to be seen.

"Can I help you?" The woman at the wheel turned to face me and I saw the resemblance at once. The same strong features with dramatic eyebrows, although this woman was older, her face softened with age. Her long, dark hair was held back at the nape of her neck, but a strand had escaped and hung down the side of her face. Her eyes held me with interest, taking in Kevin and me.

"No, I . . . well, I was just looking. Your work is very . . . nice." What a crap thing to say! I couldn't believe my ears.

She smiled and turned back to the wheel. "Looking's free. But please ask your son not to touch. It's difficult for them, you know. They learn about the world by touching. It's like asking us adults to listen to music with our ears stopped up."

It was true. Kevin was desperately trying to get at the bowls, for the glazes were colourful and had caught his eye. I gave him a biscuit to change his focus. It never fails. If there's food around, Kevin forgets about the rest of the planet.

"He's cute," the woman said. "What's his name?"

"Kevin. I'm David."

"I'm Lynne."

"You made all this stuff?"

She nodded.

"What's that?"

"A vase." The cylinder was growing in her hands, then, with a deft movement, she widened the base and made a flange at the lip.

Kevin was watching too, agog. He had abandoned his biscuit and was clearly as keen as I to get his hands into that lovely, mucky clay. Keeping him in my arms was about as much as I could manage.

I was about to give up and leave, when the woman, who'd been watching him with an amused expression on her face, wiped her hands on her apron and said, "Tell you what. I'll ask my daughter to look after him for a moment while you look around in peace. If he'll go to her, that is."

Before I could say a word, she'd gone over to a door at the opposite end of the room, which led out into a courtyard and called, "Jill! Tamsyn! Come see who I've just met."

Jill appeared in the doorway with Tamsyn on her hip. She was barefoot now and I could see the shape of her legs silhouetted through her skirt.

"Darling, meet David. And Tamsyn, this is Kevin."

I guffawed loudly, hoping that Jill's expression wasn't as hostile as it looked and said, "Goodness me, we've met before! Isn't that a strange coincidence!" I turned to Lynne for support. "We were in the library together not fifteen minutes ago!"

Jill wasn't taken in, I could see, but Lynne smiled encouragingly.

"Why don't you go through to the courtyard," she said. "Jill, honey, won't you look after Kevin for a moment, while David has a look around?"

Jill glared at her, but turned and led the way. My confidence collapsed.

"Please, it's OK, I can see you're busy," I blustered, following her.

She ignored me and sat down at a wooden table in the middle of a courtyard overflowing with potted plants, Tamsyn on her knee. She didn't offer me a seat, so I leaned against the wall.

"You're not from here," she said.

"No. Look, I'm sorry, I didn't mean your mother . . ."

"It's OK. It's not every day that a boy follows Tamsyn home from the library." Her eyes challenged me, slightly mocking. I didn't know where to look.

"It must be nice to live in a small place." Something to say, something neutral enough.

Jill shrugged. "It's too small," she said.

"Too small for what?"

"Too small for . . . privacy."

Was that code for: "Get out of here"? I felt my tenuous foothold slipping. What if I fell? I could see the headlines: "Man Falls to his Death While

Attempting to Relate to Woman". No. I must give it a better go.

"Well, Cape Town's big, but I don't get much privacy there either." I was thinking about my room, the destroyed books, my mother fighting with Trevor. "I think the most private place I've been is when I'm shooting rapids, when I've been all alone in the wilds." Surely that would impress her.

"Oh, I'm not talking about that kind of privacy. I'm talking about everyone knowing your business."

"Oh. Yeah. I know what you mean." What business? I wanted to ask. Tell me too. "Well, you don't exactly get away from that in the city either." I was thinking about the kids at school, how they teased me about my mother's new boyfriend, about her being old and pregnant. "People are cruel wherever you go."

"I thought you might like some tea." Lynne brought through a tray. "You're not in a hurry, are you?"

I shook my head. "Not at all."

My biggest immediate problem was that Kevin was struggling in my arms, trying to get hold of some nearby wind chimes. But Lynne knew the trick and diverted him with a piece of apple.

"So, what are you doing in Knysna?" asked Jill.

"I've come here to start a new life. Kevin here, he's my henchman. We're the last of the great lollipop thieves. I recycle them at night." To my immense relief, Jill smiled. "No, actually, I've got this temporary job, playing music at the Lagoonside Hotel until I can find something better."

"Where're you from?" asked Lynne.

"Cape Town. Things didn't work out for Kev and me there."

"You're a single parent too?"

Who else was she referring to? Herself or Jill? I still hadn't figured out where Tamsyn fitted in.

"Yup."

It wasn't exactly a lie. I could see they were interested. I wasn't going to show my whole hand just yet. While they were guessing about me and my life back in Cape Town, I could still get some mileage.

"Can you recommend a child-minder for Kev? One that would also be prepared to work nights."

"Why nights?" asked Jill.

"Well, I've got this job that's basically lunch-times and nights. Every day except Sundays. Kev would be sleeping nights, he never wakes up, so he'd be no problem at all. I just can't take him with me to work."

Lynne exchanged a glance with her daughter that I couldn't read. Then she turned to me.

"Maybe," she said, "we could ask Nompumelelo. She looks after Tamsyn, when Jill is helping me in the shop. But that's during the day. Nights would be a problem."

Jill's face had darkened at this suggestion.

"Mum!" she objected. "They didn't get on that well in the library."

"Nonsense!" said her mother. "Babies this age have no social sense at all! They have to learn to get on, it's not something that comes naturally! Anyway, we could just try it out. It would cut down on costs for us and give Nompumelelo more income at the same time. If it doesn't work out, it doesn't work out, no hard feelings?" She put this to me as a question.

"Of course not, that would be great!" I exclaimed, caught.

"Nompumelelo's at the hospital today, but come around tomorrow and you can meet her. If you paid her ten rand an hour over and above what we pay?"

"Sure! That's fine!" I hadn't done my sums yet, but that sounded manageable.

Without a word, Jill stood up abruptly, picked up Tamsyn and went into the house at the back of the shop. What was wrong? Had I said something?

Lynne sighed. "Don't worry about her. It's me she's angry with, not you. I'll speak to her. She'll come round."

"You sure? I mean, I don't want to cause any problems . . ."

Lynne nodded her head firmly. "It'll be fine. See you tomorrow."

As Kev and I walked back to the library, I could feel my heart sinking. Jill disliked me. She didn't want this arrangement, that was plain. And practically speaking, the arrangement wouldn't solve my major problem: what to do with Kevin at night. But it would be a start. And it was a way to get to see Jill. If she knew me better, surely she would change her mind? On the other hand, perhaps I'd better forget the whole thing.

"What d'ya say Kev? D'ya wanna go back there?" Kev was bouncing along on my shoulders, a million miles high.

"Go! Go!" he shouted. "Go!"

Yes, but which way? I thought. I'm lost in the great desert of life with an oasis in sight. Question is, is it a mirage? Can you drink a reflection of the sky?

Eleven

"Where the hell were you?" Rudd was pacing up and down in front of the library. I'd quite forgotten we'd arranged to meet there at four.

"I went on a wild goose chase," I said. "I fell in love in the library."

Rudd's eyes widened. "Wow. Was it the goose that was wild, or the chase?"

"Neither, actually. I'd say it's the gander that's wild. Wild with unrequited love."

Rudd put an arm around me. "I know what it's like. I've been there. Often. What this calls for is a bottle of wine on the beach, with a view of the sun going down."

Sitting on the small beach at the Heads with the evening colours shifting in the sky above the lagoon and a glass of red did make me feel better. It also made me feel worse. Everything was so beautiful it made my heart ache. I wanted to spend the evening with someone of the opposite sex who understood me, someone who wasn't trying to give me advice.

"The trouble with you, David," said Rudd, "is

that you think you know what's going on, but it's all head stuff. You haven't got any real experience. Now, if it had been me, I would've asked her out. You've got to take chances in this game. To use your crummy metaphor, you've got to shoot the rapid. If you hesitate too long, the rapid shoots you."

I shook my head. "Rudd, much as you're a buddy of the best calibre, you talk a load of bull. You weren't there! She was totally intimidating. There were so many negative vibes in the air, my skin got corrugations. No offence, but I'm more sensitive than you. I know when it's a no-go area."

Rudd banged his hand on his forehead. "Y'know, I can't believe what I'm hearing! This is the only area in your life where you bum out at the first sign of a challenge. What d'you expect, plain sailing? Plain sailing, as you're well aware, is plain boring. OK, trying doesn't always pay off, it takes all types, etcetera, but don't give in at the first sign of resistance!

"Anyway, how d'you know it was you she was pissed off with? She probably ate too much grapefruit for breakfast and was struggling with the most humungous heartburn, or she had a dentist appointment that afternoon, or she hates her mother. It could be anything! It's not necessarily got anything to do with you, you jerk!"

He had a point.

"Anyway, what really matters is that I still haven't sorted out what to do about child care for Kevin."

Rudd threw his hands into the air in exaggerated despair. "Y'know, one day I'm going to have to wean you off babies so you can graduate to chicks."

Before I could whip up a witty retort, Kevin threw sand in my face. I found myself scolding him severely and immediately felt guilty.

What was I going to do for this child of mine? How could I provide for him, care for him? I felt too young for this, too small myself. A new life stretched out like some uncharted sea, where a storm could whip up in a second, wash you overboard. Suddenly, I realised that I was Kevin's boat; I had to be shipworthy, so that he would have the chance I didn't. But how?

Rudd didn't understand these things, he thought that the ocean was a paddling pool.

"So whacha gonna do?"

"About what?"

"About child care? And a place to stay?"

That was the other problem. Rudd was going to be put up in the shoddy accommodation provided by the hotel but a mere musician wasn't offered that as an option. Besides, Kevin couldn't have stayed there.

Camping would be too expensive with just Kev and me and the camp-site was too far from town.

I sipped my wine, keeping an eye on Kevin at the water's edge and watched as my idea slowly surfaced. I recognised then what I'd had in mind all this time, before I'd even got to Knysna. Now I'd painted myself into a corner from where I had to admit it.

"I'm going to stay with my father," I said.

Rudd looked at me in astonishment. "Your father!" he said. "I'd forgotten that he lives . . .! You scheming bastard!"

"Well, he was here when last I heard of him. He owes me one. Probably twenty."

For the first time in my life, I realised my father had essentially done to me what my mother had done to Kevin. And for the first time, I located an anger, somewhere deep in my belly, an ancient cold feeling.

Let's see what kind of a boat he's offering now, I thought.

It wasn't difficult finding out where he stayed. All I knew about him was that he'd been living in Knysna for some years and worked with wood. So I went into a shop that sold furniture and asked if anyone knew Anthony Driver. I was directed up a hill at the back of town, to a number 18 Derry Road.

I went through an old wooden gate and knocked

on the door of the cottage. There was no answer, so I wandered around to the back, where there was a shed-cum-garage, also shut up. Kevin and I peered through the window and saw that it was obviously being used as a workshop. There was a sign in the window that said, "Back in ten minutes". So Kevin and I sat down to wait.

Kevin was showing the first signs of attempting to walk. For some time now he'd been pulling himself up on to his feet; then, toes white and tense with the effort of gripping the ground, he would stand upright, wobbling, and look about for the inevitable signals of approval before crashing to the earth.

He did so now, pulling himself up with the aid of a garden tap, but, at that moment, a black and white cat appeared, jumping gracefully down from the garden wall.

With a shriek of excitement, Kevin forgot all about the constraints of gravity and launched out across the garden on his two pins. The cat took one horrified look at the out of control menace careering towards him and fled, whereupon Kevin bit the dust, literally, then sat there wailing with disappointment and humiliation.

But I'd seen the trick. It was like learning to ride a bike. While you're thinking about what you're doing, it's impossibly difficult, but as soon as your attention shifts, hey presto, you're doing the impossible!

There must be a metaphor for life here, I thought. If I'm trying so hard to impress Jill, I'll fall flat on my face, but if I just focus on something other than her for a moment, maybe I'll get it, whatever "it" is.

And my father? What was I trying to do with him? The longer I sat on the step in the sun, waiting, the more my feet wanted to leave.

He had rejected me once before, no, not once, he'd rejected me every day of my life since I was about five, birthdays included, pretending that I didn't exist, not caring whether I lived or died. And here I was, setting myself up for it again, coming to him for help. He'd had no interest in helping me before, why should he now? I hadn't seen him in over six years, he might be married now, or have a child of his own, or he might hate children. How could I bring Kevin here, to this place where children are not wanted and ask my father to want him? This was a big mistake. I was willingly climbing into a leaking boat.

"Kevin!" I called. "Let's get out of here."

The cat had reappeared much to Kevin's delight and he objected loudly about being robbed of the opportunity to chase it again. I headed off down the road with Kevin announcing to the world what a ruthless bastard I was.

A combi drew up next to me. A familiar face at the driver's window.

"Hallo!" It was Lynne. "You coming to meet Nompumelelo?"

I nodded.

"Want a lift?"

I got in the back with Kevin, careful not to sit where Lynne could see my face in the rear view mirror. I was in a dark mood still. I held Kevin close, tried to shush him, but it was as though he could sense something going on and he refused to be quiet.

"What's the matter?" Lynne's hair was in a French plait, that stubborn strand coming down next to her eye. The tiny lines on her face like a map of her feelings. Who was she referring to? She couldn't think that I was about to discuss myself!

"Kevin wanted to demolish a cat," I said. "I predicted that he'd come off second best and intervened."

Lynne laughed and turned into the main road. "You live up there?" she asked. "No," I said, thinking of my father's cottage, how I would've loved to live there. "My father lives there."

I hadn't meant to say it. In fact, I'd decided to forget that I'd ever had a father. But despite myself, it came out.

"My ex-father," I corrected myself. "We're divorced."

Lynne was pulling into a parking bay. She turned in her seat and looked at me. "You've had a fight?"

I shook my head, averting my eyes, hating her attention. "We've never been close enough to have a fight," I said. "It doesn't matter."

Lynne sighed. "Jill and I fight all the time nowadays. It's tough, you know, being a parent."

"But did you want to?" I asked.

Lynne looked at me quizzically. "Did I want to what?"

"Did you want to be a parent?"

She threw her head back and laughed. "Sure! Don't misunderstand me. It's just that you have to learn all the time how to do it. Being the parent of a one-year-old is very different from being the parent of a twenty-year-old!"

"Well, I think Jill is lucky to have you."

She looked pleased. "Well, I'm lucky to have her too." She looked at me probingly. "Who is your father, David?"

I'd started to feel more comfortable while the conversation was focused on them. Now her question made me panic. What if she knew him? I didn't even want him to know I was in town. Either he wouldn't want to see me, which would be awful, or else he'd feel it was his duty to see me, which would be even worse.

"It doesn't matter," I said. "Our relationship is over. It's been over for about fifteen years. I'd rather forget about it."

She continued to look at me, my feeling of discomfort growing, so I got out of the car, saying, "I'd like to meet Nompumelelo."

Jill was helping a customer and didn't even look my way as we entered the shop. Lynne took me through to their living quarters behind the shop, walking first through the courtyard overflowing with potted plants and through a door into a playroom.

Tamsyn looked up from the blocks she was busy with on the floor and pointed at Kevin. "Baba!" she announced.

Lynne picked her up. "Yes, my darling, the baba has come to play with you."

Kevin had staggered over to the myriad of toys lying strewn all over the floor and was going through a selection process with his mouth. A woman came through from the kitchen.

"Hi, Nompumelelo," said Lynne. "This is the young man I was telling you about. His name is Kevin."

Nompumelelo beamed. "Hallo, Mischief! Come to Lelo!" She swept him off the ground and into her well-cushioned embrace. Kevin regarded her with astonishment.

"Hi," I said. "I'm David." We shook hands, African style and I also fell under the wide beam of her smile.

"I'll look after your baby. I know about babies. I've had five of my own!"

I liked her easy flowing manner instantly. We agreed to try it out for half an hour to see how he settled in, so I went down town to a restaurant and had a cup of coffee.

I sat there with my heart sinking. It was all a dream, it was all a stupid fantasy. I must be crazy to think it was as easy as that, just to walk away from my old life, bringing Kevin with me.

If I were an explorer and I'd got this far, if I'd left my home and comforts and back-packed to the bottom of Everest, my next step would be to set up base camp. But how to do that? I had little money, no real qualifications, a temporary job which paid abominably, nowhere to stay and no child care.

If I didn't come up with something fast, I would have to go back to Cape Town. The thought of that made me go cold. Trevor would say, "I told you so!" in his sneering, supercilious, drunken way. He would be mad at me anyway. I'd promised to phone him to let him know how Kev and I were doing, but I hadn't. I couldn't bear him to be checking up on me, I couldn't stand to waste even one measly cent on a phone call to him.

If I were on my own, I could make it, but with Kevin it was a different ball game. He needed baby food and clean nappies, clothes and somewhere safe and warm and loving. We were both pioneers, of a kind, but Kev wasn't old enough for me to take too many risks on his behalf.

I sat on that restaurant chair feeling stuck, unable to move forward and unable to go back. I knew if I went back to Cape Town, Kevin would be put into foster care. I had to find a way through.

I walked slowly back to the shop.

Kevin was having a whale of a time. He and Tamsyn were sitting at a small table, up to their eyebrows in yoghurt.

"He's a little monkey, this one," said Nompumelelo with a smile. "He knows what he wants!"

It could have been great. Things could have worked out, if it wasn't for money. Without money, you couldn't explore the world, you couldn't even save a child.

I realised suddenly that Nompumelelo was looking at me expectantly. She wanted to know whether she had the job. How to tell her? That I don't even earn enough to rent a roof over my head, let alone hire someone to look after my child.

"So, David? What d'you think? Will it work out for you and Kev?" Lynne had entered the room behind me and behind her came another man, tall and bearded.

At first, against the light, I couldn't make out his features, then my heart nearly stopped. It was my father. I didn't know what to say. I just stared at him as he glanced towards me, then our eyes locked. His eyes widened perceptibly as he recognised me.

"This is a long ten minutes," I blurted out. It was the only thing I could think of saying.

"What d'you mean?"

"The sign. In your window. 'Back in ten minutes'."

He gave a half-smile. "Oh, that. Well, time in Knysna is different. You obviously haven't been here long enough to work that out."

I couldn't believe this conversation. I felt the coldness at my centre, I wanted to walk right out of the room. The bastard hadn't seen me for six years and all he could talk about was the sign in his window!

Lynne was looking in astonishment from Anthony to myself and back again.

"You two know each other?" she said.

As he started to nod, I interjected, "No, not at all."

Anthony looked at me with an expression that I couldn't read, but that made me uncomfortable.

"Well, I'd better be going then," I said, whipping

Kevin out of his chair and getting yoghurt down my front. "Thanks, Lynne, thanks Nompumelelo. I'll drop in some other time when you don't have company."

I headed to the door but Anthony barred my way.

"Hey," he said. "Not so fast. If you took the trouble to come up to my place to see me, why're you leaving in such a hurry? And who's this chappie here?" He ruffled Kevin's scant hair.

I stared into his eyes, eyes that resembled mine, eyes that were closed to me and said, "This is my child."

"Good God!" exclaimed Lynne. "I've only seen it now! Anthony's your father, right?"

"Wrong," I said. "Anthony *was* my father only in that he forgot to use a condom."

There was a shocked silence, but Anthony took only a moment to recover.

"Looks like you forgot to use one too," he said.

"Wrong again," I retorted, infuriated to see a smile in the corner of Lynne's mouth. How dare he humiliate me like this!

"I gather you two haven't seen each other for a long time," said Lynne. "Shall we sit down and have a cup of tea?"

"No. Thanks. I've got to go." Without another look at any of them, I left.

Twelve

"I can't believe you just walked out!" Rudd was being his usual helpful self. "I mean, there was your chance and you blew it!"

"Rudd, you're on another planet! This is more complicated than you think. For starters, my father, in fact everyone in Knysna, thinks that Kev is my son."

"Hasn't your Dad met Kevin before?"

"Nope. I told you. He hasn't been around for twelve years."

"So, you have two choices. Either you carry on with the fabrication, or you tell him the truth."

"I can't tell Anthony that Kev is my half-brother! You don't realise how much my parents hate each other! He would only see Kevin as the son of Tracey, he wouldn't see him for the lovely child he is."

At that moment, Kev staggered past, his laden nappy working its way down towards his ankles. Rudd mock-fainted, clutching at his throat, making gurgling noises. Kevin stopped and watched, fascinated.

"You call that reek lovely?"

I kicked his butt and scrambled after Kev, who was earnestly zooming in on the neighbour's fire.

We only continued on that topic later, once we'd eaten and Kevin had passed out on a blanket next to the fire. I took out my guitar and sang to a sky flung with stars, I sang to the soft, warm light of a camp-fire on a baby's face, I sang to a dream lost.

"I disagree with you," interrupted Rudd. The more depressed I became at my predicament, the more cheerful he waxed. "You said yourself, your dad owes you. Y'know what? You're so scared of failure, you haven't even tried yet. I bet your dad would fancy being a grandaddy!"

"Just shut up, will you? I happen to know my father better than you. I also happen not to be scared of failure, it's just I don't particularly relish giving him my face so he can kick my teeth in."

"You don't need to do that. You've already kicked yourself in the teeth."

"Very funny."

"You've got to consider all the options, man."

"Yeah. Well, forget that one. Got any others?"

Rudd thought for a moment. "I think you should phone Trevor. And your mother. They should give you money for the kid. They should pay you maintenance. Then you'd have more to go on."

I snorted. "Ask Trevor for money! You must be

joking! One of his reasons for putting Kevin into foster care was that he doesn't *have* any money. And my mother's vanished. And broke, going by her last phone call. Anyway, even if Trevor did cough up, he'd use it against me for the rest of my life. He'd say it was another reason why I was unfit to look after Kevin."

Rudd shook his head and sighed. "Jees, you've got an answer for everything. So whatcha gonna do?"

I had a sudden vision of Kev and me in the gutter.

"I'm going to have to go back to Cape Town," I said. "I'll tell Lynne and Nompumelelo and the Hotel in the morning. We'll get the bus back."

Rudd stared at me. "You're a stubborn bastard," he said.

We sat silent for a while, pooled by the light of the fire, wrapped in our own thoughts, then Rudd changed tack.

"We could rob a bank, or mug old ladies," he suggested. "If it's just money you need, there're other ways of getting it." He mused for a while. "Or you could start a playschool. A camping adventure for under-two's. You're good at this," he said, indicating Kevin. "I'll hand out leaflets at the hotel to all frazzled parents who come in to rejuvenate themselves on gin and tonics. 'Have a real holiday! Dump your kid on David. No more sleepless nights, no more vomit and poo, no more mysterious icky messes on the linoleum.

Waterski peacefully, dance the night away with your mind at rest, knowing that little Jonny isn't drowning and little Suzie hasn't been abducted. And breastfeeding mothers, don't miss this special offer: Rudd will help you to express breast milk for your baby in the privacy of your own bedroom!'"

"You're sick," I said, smiling despite myself.

"Thanks for the compliment. Why is it that in this relationship, I'm the one with all the good ideas? Now, all you would need is a large and empty swimming pool. You just stick the kids in there and throw in food every couple of hours. And when they get too messy, you just stand on the side and hose them down."

"Rudd, I recommend that you think twice before having children."

"You're damn right! In fact, I'll only have to think once. Only problem is, babies aren't made from thinking. Didn't your mother ever teach you that?"

That night I had a dream which woke me up it was so intense. I lay burning in my sleeping bag, the sounds of Rudd and Kevin breathing beside me and thought about it over and over.

I was looking for my father and found myself in a dark house, alone and very cold. I couldn't see which way to go, or how to get out.

I came to a dimly-lit and narrow stairway which led down into the ground. I followed it, even though I was terrified of going down into an enclosure. The stairs were huge and I could barely descend from one to the next. I knew it would be difficult to get out if there was danger.

Then the dream changed and I was standing in a room. I was very tiny, a child and naked. Much to my embarrassment, Lynne was in the room, fully dressed.

I wanted to explain to her that I had lost my clothes, but before I could, she'd picked me up and put me on the table. Then she started to work on my body, moulding first my face, then my arms and legs, then my torso.

Under her firm, strong hands, I could feel myself bursting with pleasure, weak with it. Then I began to get scared. It felt as though she could do anything with me, she was too big, I was too little. I thought she might be preparing to eat me.

It was at that moment that I woke up, still burning with desire, but filled with confusion too, at my fear of her. It had felt so real that I wondered how I was ever going to see her again. I wouldn't, I thought. I'd phone. I'd phone the next morning, before leaving town.

Damn it, I thought. She knew my father all the time. How did they know each other? Could they be having a scene? Then I felt guilty. I'd been attracted to Jill, but I was having erotic nightmares about her mother! And I didn't even know either of them well!

I lay there, confused and miserable, unable to sleep. After a couple of hours of tossing and turning, I'd had enough. I got dressed and went out into the night. I'll just take a quick walk down the road, I thought. Get my body tired, change my focus.

The night was stunning and still but for the crickets and the soft shush of a warm breeze in the trees. A moon saucered in the sky just above the lagoon. Amazing to think that people have walked on that, I thought. Amazing to think of a rocket on its way to other planets in our solar system, travelling for years, loaded with electronic eyes, feeding information back to scientists who are busy getting divorces. What was it that that guy Mindell wrote? That we know more about space travel than how to get along with each other.

I thought of my mother, how I loved and hated her, how she'd eat me up, then spit me out, how I'd tried so hard, but was never quite good enough. And my father, that cold, hard place of waiting, that unknown territory fenced and barred, with signs saying: "Keep out, trespassers will be prosecuted".

I'd never been kept out by a sign like that before. Imagine wanting to cross the Gobi desert on foot and coming to fenced land that said "Keep out"! Would I pack up the expedition and go home? If it was my father's land, I would. That was the sad truth.

No, the really sad truth was it was my father who'd had a chance, he was the one who'd blown it. Yesterday he couldn't even touch me. What if he touches Lynne? The thought made me go cold, then hot with an unidentifiable feeling; it made me walk faster, breathe harder.

Lynne. She was old enough to be my mother! Yet I recognised that the looks that attracted me to Jill were more refined in Lynne, that she was a more attractive person to me. I thought of what Rudd would say, that it was my own mother I was missing, that I should have my head read. Not that I would ever mention this to him. Not that there would be any cause to mention it at all.

The dark road pushed past; my mind and feet were walking the same treadmill, round and round. My life stretched before me like a road full of potholes, great chunks torn out, no map, dangers lurking. I remembered a dream where even the road had tilted, threatening to throw me into the void.

My angel. Where was my angel? She was missing. I no longer thought of my grandmother, of the goodness she'd brought into my life. That was a childish fancy, no memory of a grandmother could help me now, no angel was going to flap down from heaven, no Superman was going to forgive me the colour of my socks.

I was on my own now, I was an adult in an adult world, with all the essentials of childhood missing, a house without foundations.

I'd always believed it was possible, that I could do it another way, that the adults I knew were just aberrations and that I didn't have to be like any of them. They kept safe and narrow, sticking their heads in their TVs, they knew more about the plot of the current soap than the mess of their own lives.

To my astonishment, I found myself on the outskirts of the town. Surely I hadn't walked that far, that quickly? What if Kevin had woken up, or Rudd? I turned back quickly, then stopped. They never did. I was the one who had to shake them awake in the mornings.

I stood there on the pavement, flooded by streetlight, struck with indecision. I knew where my feet were leading me, but I was scared to admit it. I'll just take one look, I thought. Just a last look at what might have been before reality dropped on my head like a sack of sewage.

There was a light on in the shop, I hadn't expected that. For security, must be. The curtains drawn. I went up to the shop front and put my eye to a chink in the curtains. My ears picked up the sound of the wheel – she was working! I couldn't see her, only part of the display on the opposite wall.

I'd like to buy something, I thought, something to remember her by. Something to blow my last few bucks on. That vase, it was on the shelf now, drying out next to vases of a similar shape, fired and glazed in the deepest of blues. I'd never owned a vase before. I thought of what Rudd would say: "You stupid jerk! What a waste of bloody money!" He'd try to use it as a beer mug, or something.

I thought of knocking on the door. She'd get a fright, she was working, I wouldn't know what to say. And what if Anthony was there, sitting quietly in the room watching her with soft eyes, or waiting for her in her bed.

I shifted from one foot to the other, restless with indecision. It was now or never. In the morning I'd be gone.

Her face at the window. Had I really knocked? Her smile, the door opening.

"Come in," she said. "You're also a night creature?"

"I couldn't sleep," I blustered, blushing deeply, hesitating on the threshold, trying to see past her into the shop. "I'm not . . . interrupting anything, am I? I could come back in the morning . . ."

She shook her head. "No. Come on in." Her eyes searched mine, mine didn't know where to look.

I rubbed the stubble on my face, I wished I'd shaved. I felt too young, too young for her. I followed her into the shop. She started again at the wheel, working quietly, intent and intense. Within moments, it seemed as though she'd forgotten I was there. Maybe I should go, I thought. I couldn't stand my own agitation. But there was something in watching her work that was soothing to me, something that drew me in.

I wondered how old she was. I wondered whether she'd ever even noticed me. Her hands moved and played, silky brown with wet clay. It was too hot in the shop, I was having difficulty breathing. The memory of the dream was still alive in my body, I couldn't tear my eyes away from her hands, the way they moved, milking form out of the clay. I don't know how long I sat, watching, it felt like forever, waves of hot pleasure washing through me.

At last I found my voice. "You make it look so easy," I said.

She looked up, remembered I was there, smiled.

"I love this work. I'm in a strange state of mind when I work with clay. It's very peaceful, yet intense, as though I'm involved in something . . . primal, more primal than painting even. It's like giving the earth shape. This medium is so tactile, so yielding, yet working with it, you have to pit your will against its will all the time before it reveals its secret. Looks easy, I know, but I've been working with clay for twenty years. It's only in the last few months I've felt true mastery over the form."

I hadn't yet felt true mastery over anything. Surely it didn't take that long! I reckoned she'd told me that to remind me how many years stood between us, how young I was in her eyes.

"Of course, having said that, this vase will no doubt become determined to prove me wrong!" she added.

I didn't think so. By the looks of things, this vase was just flourishing under her touch. I wanted that for myself. I suddenly saw her as an angel, one that could reveal my deepest secrets to myself, one that could show me what was missing.

Then, as though an express train had hit me, I saw what it was she was making. A vase, yes, but one that was shaped like a dick, a hard dick. It was as though I was seeing my dream.

I felt faint with disbelief. I gripped the table I was leaning against, a fever washed through me. I looked at her face, intent on her task, to see whether this was a joke, whether she was laughing at me, but she was oblivious of my discomfort. The vase was beautifully fashioned, it was no joke. It contained elements of her style, but was very different from any other piece in the shop.

Lynne finished what she was doing and wiped her hands on her apron.

"I love to work at night," she said, then must have caught something about the expression on my face, for she laughed and looked back at her work.

"D'you like it?" she asked.

She might as well have asked me whether I liked my dreams. She might as well have asked me whether I liked her.

"Yes," I gulped. "It's very . . ." I scrabbled around in my brain for an adequate adjective, "graphic. I'd like to have given something like that to my biology teacher at school."

What an inappropriate thing to say! I could've kicked myself.

"You had a crush on her?"

I groaned. "Oh, no! But she was terrified of anything below the neck."

Lynne laughed, went over to a nook and put the kettle on.

"It's a commission. There's a gallery in Johannesburg that's having an exhibition of erotica. I sell quite a lot through them."

I couldn't take my eyes off the piece.

"It'll look great with flowers in it," I remarked. I imagined a bunch of daisies bursting forth out of the opening in the glans.

Lynne looked pleased. "Yeah," she said. "Wait till you see my vulval bird baths. That's my next project. Tea or coffee?"

"Tea, please. I'm going to have to get a decent job and put money aside each month."

"Why?"

"So I can buy your work." I'd commission a vulval jacuzzi from her, fountains made in the shape of her breasts, pillows made from her hair.

She nodded, passing me a mug. "That'd be great. But why don't you make your own things?"

"Oh, I couldn't!"

"Why not?"

"I'm no good at making things. I'm only any good at doing things."

"You make music."

"That's different."

"Why?"

"Oh, I don't know. The guitar is there already and you learn the chords and then you can just play around with them. With this . . . well, you'd have to know more about what you want to do, what you're going to achieve. You have to have more ideas."

Lynne put her head to one side. "I'm not so sure.

Tell you what. I'll teach you a bit about making things out of clay if you teach me a bit about making music on the guitar." Her eyes a challenge. My breath stuck somewhere in my chest.

"Sure, yeah, well. No. I can't. I mean, I'd love to, but . . ." Hopeless waves running through, the rapid shooting me. "My plans have changed. I'm going back on the bus to Cape Town tomorrow."

Her look of surprise. "Why? Because of your father or your wife?"

My wife? Then I remembered. Kev was my son. I couldn't have done that by myself. For one wild moment, I wanted to laugh.

"No!" My voice was too loud. "My wife's dead. Killed in a car accident."

"Oh. I'm sorry."

"That's OK. It was a long time ago. I'm over it now."

Her look of surprise. Kevin . . . How old was Kevin? Only fourteen months! Oh, hell.

"I mean, it was very traumatic at the time."

Change the subject.

"No, I have to go back because . . . things aren't working out. I had a dream I thought was possible . . . but . . . things aren't that simple. That's why I came over now. I couldn't sleep and . . . well, I wanted to say thank you to you. For trying to help me get sorted out."

She was silent for a moment, holding me in her gaze. She's smelt a rat, I thought. I've lied to her and she knows it. I shifted uncomfortably against the table and sipped my tea.

"You could let your father help you," she said.

I threw my head back and laughed, falsely, hard. I suddenly felt vulnerable, exposed, as though she'd seen through me to something more important than the lie, something worse.

"He wouldn't help me if I was dying! He hasn't cared what happens to me in years!"

"You so sure that's true?"

"It is true! I should know!"

I hated to think of them discussing poor little David while they lay in each other's arms. My father was the real liar. If he'd told her that he cared for me, he was just covering his tracks, he was just trying to look good.

"He hasn't bothered to contact me in years, not even birthdays! Don't be fooled by him, Lynne! He hates me!"

I wanted to get a knife in, somehow. If I couldn't have Lynne, my father wasn't going to have her either. I had to make Lynne see what a bastard he was.

"Look, David, I don't know what's happened between the two of you and I don't know either of you well. I'm sure Anthony has made mistakes. But give him a chance. Give yourself a chance."

"You saw how he brushed me aside yesterday! Why should *I* be the one to give *him* a chance? He should be grovelling after me!"

"Sure. Maybe. Maybe he would do that if he knew where you're staying."

She didn't understand a thing.

"Listen, Lynne. He's known where I've been staying for the past nineteen years of my life. He's a bastard!" He'll leave you too, I wanted to add. He'll pretend to love you and then he'll leave.

"Look, I know this is more complicated than I realise, but you're talking about your dream. You said so yourself. When you've got a dream, you have to follow it. To the ends of the earth. Through hell and back again. You've got to follow it until you know there's no more energy in it, until your focus shifts. If you don't, it gets stored up somewhere inside, it goes stale and old and mouldy and sour. Then it starts to make you sick."

She was leaning towards me, she took my hands in hers. I realised how cold I was, how warm she was, how my hands were somehow attached to my body, how close I was to drowning. How she was talking my language, the language of pioneers.

She smiled. "I know what I'm talking about. My dream is to learn how to play the guitar."

I couldn't do it. While she was holding my

hands, while I was fixed in her gaze, while she was asking me to stay, I couldn't keep the wall hard, I couldn't keep her out. *This* is my dream, I wanted to tell her. But my father already has my dream. I can't stay in this town and have my father take this away from me in front of my eyes.

"I'm staying at the Heads' Caravan Park," I told her. "I'm leaving tomorrow. Please tell Nompumelelo I'm sorry. And Jill. Say goodbye to Jill and Tamsyn."

It's now or never, I thought. Her face is still close, her face is still open to me. If I kiss her now, at least I'll have that.

Lynne nodded and stood up. "Let me give you a lift," she said. "The sun's coming up."

The sky outside the shop was whitening at the edges.

I shook my head. The moment had passed. She was wrong. This was a dream that had passed me by. This was the cold house, this was the feeling of being lost. The wall hardened.

"No, thanks," I said. "I like to walk."

As it was, I managed to hitch a ride back on an early morning bread truck. Rudd and Kevin were still asleep when I got back to the tent. I started to pack.

Thirteen

"C'mon! We've got to get moving!" I felt exasperated. Rudd was floundering around in his sleeping bag, Kevin was unpacking my rucksack. At this rate we'd miss the bus.

"Stop that, Kev! Put the clothes in there!"

"Inthere!" agreed Kevin, pulling more stuff out of the rucksack.

"Damn it!" I raged, grabbing the rucksack from him. "You're too much work, Kev! I said stop it!"

Kev's little face widened with contrition, then he released a loud wail.

"Shut up, the two of you!" moaned Rudd. "I'm trying to get some sleep!"

"Rudd! You're doing this on purpose! The bus passes through some time this morning, I'm not even sure when and at this rate I'm going to miss it."

"What's the rush? Catch the damn thing tomorrow!"

"I'll tell you what the rush is!" I warned. "The rush is that if you don't move your butt, I'm going to take Kevin's nappy off and sit him on your head."

Rudd's face emerged from the neck of his sleeping bag, creased with sleep.

"Now that's not a very nice thing to say." He put on a posh accent. "Besides demonstrating that you are a man of brutal methods, it displays an attempt to evade the essential question. So, in the pursuit of truth, I ask again: What's the rush?"

The rush was that I was worried that Lynne might take it into her head to tell my father where I was staying and that my father might take it into his head to come over. What would happen then was anyone's guess, but I didn't plan to be around to witness it.

"By the way, where were you last night?" he asked.

"Losing at roulette. Doing the mayor's wife. And robbing the bank. Like you told me. That's why I'm in a hurry to leave town. Now, move it, damn you!"

At last I managed to get the show on the road. Rudd was unusually silent as we drove into town. So was I. I stared out of the car window at the lagoon, close to tears. My father hadn't come. He didn't care. I'd been right. The dream was over.

As we turned into the main road to town, we saw the intercity bus coming down the hill behind us. I'd had half a mind to hitch if we'd missed the bus, but I was concerned to do this safely, for Kevin's sake.

Still, it didn't seem right. Explorers just didn't go by bus.

At the bus stop, Rudd gave me a hug.

"You look after that kid," he said. "You just talk to Trevor, sort something out."

I hugged him back. For all his bullshit, he was a great guy.

"Have a good time, Rudd," I said. "I'll see you back in town."

He turned to go.

"And Rudd!"

"Yeah?"

"Don't get pregnant!"

He smiled, then his face dropped. "You didn't let the Lagoonside management know!"

The bus was waiting.

"Please, tell them from me. Say I drowned. Or that I fell on a bus. Or I lost my voice. Or . . . yeah, that's it! Tell them I lost my father!"

"Hallo, David." A hand on my shoulder. My father.

I lost my voice.

"Hallo, Mr Driver. It is Mr Driver?" Rudd, all smiles. They shook hands. "I'm Rudd. I'm the one who's saved your son from being a total jerk. Because of me he now has reasonable taste in music and chicks, although he still has a way to go with humour. He's got a terrible sense of humour. Look, the cosmos has just played a joke on him and I bet he's not even going to smile!"

He gesticulated in the direction of the bus, which was disappearing down the main road in the direction of Cape Town, my rucksack on board. I looked at Rudd. I wanted to hit him, but I had Kevin on one arm and my guitar in the other.

"All gone!" said Kev in delight. "All gone!"

"That's it!" I said to Rudd, angrily ignoring my father. "Get me on that bus!"

"I've got a better idea," said Rudd, dodging me. "I'll go get that rucksack." He jumped into his car and sped off like the original car chase.

Anthony and I looked at each other. "Let's go home," he said.

Turned out that the intercity bus goes faster than Rudd's car and it took him till George, three stops later, to catch up with it. Then they were reluctant to give my rucksack to him, but at last he persuaded them, that although I'd bought a ticket five minutes before the bus left and put my luggage on the bus, I had in fact changed my mind and that I was not hiding on the bus, pretending not to be on it.

"Morons," he said. "If that bus company was running the country, no-one would ever be able to change their mind."

"I *hadn't* changed my mind!" I objected.

"Of course you had," he said. "Only you didn't know it yet." He wiped his plate clean with his burger roll and leaned back in his seat. "So what happened?"

My father had taken me back to his place and offered me something to eat. I was still furious and confused.

"What did you do that for?" I'd asked.

"What?"

"You made me miss the bus."

"I didn't. I just wanted to see you."

I glared at him. "Lynne shouldn't have bothered," I said. "It had nothing to do with her."

He stared at me. "This has got nothing to do with Lynne. Why did you come to Knysna, David?"

"It wasn't to see you."

He sighed. "Then why did you come up here?"

I stood up and went to stand near the door. I wanted to get out of there. It was too painful, this interrogation. What gave him the right?

"You know, I've been waiting so long for this," he said.

I stared at him. "For what?"

"For you to show some indication that you want me in your life."

I couldn't believe my ears. "What child has to ask a parent to show them some affection?"

"You aren't a child any more, David."

I turned on him. "Oh, so all these years it's been my fault! I didn't ask you into my life, so you had every right to stay away!"

He shook his head sadly. "No, it's not like that."

"Well, what on earth do you mean, then? What were you waiting for? For me to come grovelling to you? Tell me! What were you waiting for?"

"What's happened, David? Please tell me? Why did you come to Knysna?"

"You want that, don't you! You want me to be in some kind of trouble! Well, I'm not! I'm just starting a life of my own. I'm past needing parents that don't want me, I don't need anything from you!" It was Lynne who'd done this, she'd thought I was in trouble, she'd told Anthony. "All I need is for you to get out of my way when I'm boarding a bus!"

Anthony was looking at me in a strange kind of way, as though he was struggling with something. I couldn't bear it, the look on his face.

"Damn it, you don't give me a chance!" he said.

I remembered that phrase, he'd used it on my mother.

I was about to walk out, when he said something that made me stop, which made me feel I didn't know what to do.

"David. I need you."

I kicked the threshold of the door, wanting to leave, wanting to hear more. The garden was bright outside. Kevin was out there, a lovely child in my father's garden, innocently pulling up all the flowers. Let him do it, I thought. Behind me was my father, in a cold house.

"Please. Sit down. I need to explain something to you. Then I'll drive you to Cape Town, if you want."

Reluctantly I took a seat and looked at his plates stacked on a shelf. Wondered who'd made them. Wondered who this man was.

Anthony sat quietly, digging in the sugar as though looking for the right words.

"I was wrong," he said. "I was young, then. I didn't know any better." He looked at me, then indicated out into the garden. "Looks like you do. So I can't only blame my youth."

He scratched his beard, folded his arms.

"Look," he began again. "I don't want to blame what happened on your mother."

Yes you do, I thought. Of course you do.

"When it all fell apart, you were only a year old. I loved you David, you were a part of me, but at that age you were more a part of Tracey. She'd suckled you, she'd grown you in her belly. She wanted to keep you, she said. She wanted me out of her life and out of yours. She said she wouldn't grant visiting rights, she

129

said I wasn't fit to be a father. And much as I wanted you, I knew she'd win any custody battle and that for me to get even visiting rights would mean taking her to court, with all that entailed.

"I decided against it. I thought I'd wait until you were older, then you could decide for yourself whether you wanted me for a dad. But it was too painful. I did get to see you every now and then, when I was in Cape Town, at first I made sure I'd see you, even though it meant seeing your mother, the inevitable fights and seeing her with her new lover. But it was just too painful. You acted like I was a stranger."

"But you were a stranger! What did you expect! That wasn't my fault!"

He nodded, his mouth tense. "I know. Meanwhile, I had another life, away from all that, here, where I could forget. Then one day, I heard you were staying with Tracey's mother. After all Tracey had gone through to ensure that I didn't get near you, she gave you to her mother!"

"You never came after that."

"I know. I never liked her . . . But I knew that she was kind to you and better for you than either Tracey or I'd ever been. So I thought, well, that's for the best."

"Look!"

Through the door toddled Kevin, bunches of uprooted flowers in his hands, beaming delightedly. I glanced quickly at Anthony. Just lay one hand on him, I thought, just one hard word and I'll get you.

A look of alarm crossed Anthony's face and he leapt out of his chair.

"Kevin," he said. "Those are my flowers!"

"Mine!" said Kevin fiercely, clutching the broken stems tightly to his chest and running to hide behind me. Anthony looked at me appealingly. I pretended this wasn't happening. I wanted to see what he would do.

Anthony stood in the middle of the floor, scratching his beard. Then he went down on his haunches and said in his most reasonable and appealing voice, "Tell you what, Kevin, those flowers need to live in the ground. Come outside with me and we can plant them again."

"No! Mine!" shrieked Kevin, wedging himself in behind my chair.

I don't blame him, I thought. I want beauty in my life too. I also want to break the rules.

Anthony looked so powerless, crouched on the floor in front of me, I wanted to laugh, I wanted to tip him over. He's mine! I wanted to say, this beautiful child who can stand up to you and take what he wants from you, from life.

"All right," said Anthony lamely. "You can have them. But I'm going out into the garden right now and I'm going to plant some more. If you want to, you can come and help me."

"More!" yelled Kevin gleefully, flinging down the flowers and rushing through the door.

Anthony smiled at me wryly and picked up the mess of vegetation.

"I can see that he's a child after your own heart," he said.

Fourteen

My own heart. What did he know about my own heart? All these years Tracey'd told me what a bastard he was and to prove her point there'd been no sign of him and now? Now this stranger, this flesh and blood, tells me it was different from what I thought, asks me to forgive him.

I'll take my time, I thought. I'll make him suffer.

In the meantime we moved in. Anthony said Kev and I could use the loft above his house. I insisted on paying a nominal rent. It was a token of something important. I could keep my distance from him and I wouldn't owe him anything. At the same time I was getting back my due. My overdue.

"You comfortable up here?" he asked, standing at the entrance, which was situated at the top of an outside staircase.

The loft was just great; rudimentary, but comfortable enough. Kevin would have to brush up on his mountaineering abilities to get up the stairs, though. But he'd faced worse challenges before.

I was glad to see him standing outside, not

marching in as though he owned the place. It occurred to me that he was nervous. I liked that. I didn't fancy the thought of him having all the power. It'd felt like that all these years. Never again, I thought.

"Come in," I offered magnanimously. He ducked in through the low doorway and came to sit on an old wicker chair that creaked under his weight.

He was a tall man, a little stooped, as though slightly embarrassed by his height. His face was more lined than I remembered and more tanned. Still attractive, with his beard starting to grey, with his hairline receding. Am I going to look like him when I'm his age? I wondered.

"Da!" said Kevin, waddling up to me, his face and hands smeared with a white paste. A waft of spearmint accompanied him. Toothpaste. Oh, brother. I hid my irritation at having to clean up the mess. I wanted Anthony to see what a good parent looked like.

Anthony said, "So where did this little chappy come from?"

I didn't want to get into this but it was unavoidable. What had I told Lynne?

"His mother died. It's just the two of us now."

"I'm sorry. What happened?"

"I'd rather not talk about it. It's just one of those things."

Kev was objecting strongly to my ministrations with the face-cloth.

"Just don't do it again, buddy," I warned. "He loves the taste. They should make a spearmint babyfood. It'd sell like hot cakes." I handed Kev his soft ball.

"It can't be easy being a single parent."

I shrugged. "Kev and me, we understand each other." Now was the moment. "Anthony."

"Yeah?"

"I start work tomorrow night. At the Lagoonside."

"Uh-huh?"

"Kevin needs to be somewhere safe while I'm at work. He would be sleeping, so it wouldn't be a problem."

"Uh-huh."

Come on. This is your chance. If you want reparation that badly, I'm giving you that chance. We sat and stared across the room at each other. I couldn't read his face. I took a deep breath. He wasn't going to make this easy.

"I want to leave Kevin here. With you."

Anthony looked at me, he looked at his fingernails. He looked out of the window.

"Oh," he said. "That's going to be a problem."

I waited, stony.

"Every night?"

135

I nodded. "Except Sundays."

"Well, maybe I could help you out now and then. But every night . . ." He frowned. "I have a life of my own, you know. You can't expect that of me."

The lines were drawn. He still wasn't able to extend a real helping hand. It was true what Tracey'd said. Anthony was selfish, he didn't want anything to curtail his freedom. I'd impinged too much on his life when I was a baby. So he'd left.

I shrugged. "OK," I said. "Fine."

"I have to go out now," he said abruptly, standing up and handing me a key. "Here's a key to the house. Fix yourself something to eat, if you want."

He walked to the door, then turned. "I'm glad you're going to be staying a while. I'm really glad." He hesitated a moment, as though waiting for me to say something, but when I didn't, he left.

I looked at the key. I wanted to run after him, to shout, "Where are you going?" I wanted to tail him, spy on him, find out about his life. I was afraid of what I might discover. Lynne. I dreaded her coming here, to this house, I dreaded her soft eyes for Anthony.

He'd given me a key. I wasn't interested in food, but I was interested in my father's life. I grabbed Kevin and descended the stairs.

Once inside Anthony's house I found an apple to

keep Kev busy. Then I went straight to his bedroom. Evidence. I had to find the evidence. But there were no women's panties on the floor, or in the wash-basket, or under his pillow.

In the bathroom there was only one toothbrush and no sign of cosmetics or creams. With some relief I realised she didn't sleep over here. Then what was their relationship? Maybe it wasn't too late, maybe I could save her from my father. Maybe they were just friends?

A crash from the kitchen. An open cupboard. Kevin, wailing, amidst a broken jar of lentils. Miraculously unscathed. I picked him gingerly out of the shards.

"Don't touch!" I warned.

His shocked, distraught face streaked with tears, eyes turned accusingly towards the mess on the floor.

"Don tush!" he admonished the broken jar angrily, wagging a finger.

I hugged him and wondered about making this place baby-proof.

"Bath-time," I said, lugging him off to the bathroom. I ran a shallow bath and plonked him into it with a few plastic cups and utensils from the kitchen. It was as good a playpen as any. Then I cleared up the mess, found a beer and went through Anthony's bookshelf.

You can always tell what someone's like by what you find in their bookshelves. *Routing Techniques*; *Paint Effects*. Boring. Ursula LeGuin! And James Barker! He was into science fiction. He couldn't be that bad. *The Road Less Travelled*. Hmmm. He should read that again. Love is not a feeling, remember? Love is looking after your grandson to compensate for bad parenting. Michael Ondaatjie! I'd wanted to read him. Well, well, there was hope yet.

I put Kevin to bed and began to read *The English Patient*. It took a while, but at last I managed to dissolve into the book and stop wondering where Anthony was.

"So whatcha gonna do about work?" Rudd had finished his envious inspection of my living quarters and had turned his attention to me.

"I'm going to take him with me."

Rudd stared. "You can't do that!" he said.

"Of course I can," I said uncertainly. "I'll make a bed for him somewhere out of the way. And I've bought a baby harness. I'll tie him to a table."

Rudd shook his head. "The management won't like it," he said. "He's not eighteen yet."

"You never drank underage? Anyway, I'm not about to ask the management for permission."

Rudd rolled his eyes. "I was wrong about you," he said. "You don't give up."

It was worth a try. I had no other alternative. I made sure Kevin didn't get any sleep that day and at seven o'clock I set off for the Lagoonside, with Kevin on my back, my guitar under my arm.

I didn't bother to tell Anthony I was going. Keep it cool, I thought. I still haven't forgiven you.

Kevin was grizzly and tired. And heavy. This is my life, I thought. My baby and my music. Off we go into a new adventure. I didn't feel that confident.

They didn't like it. There was a big fuss.

"This is no place for a baby," objected the guy who ran the bar. "You must be joking! It gets smoky and noisy. Who's going to be responsible if he gets stood on, or hurt? Or kidnapped?"

He's kidnapped already, I wanted to tell him. It's not likely to happen twice.

"You won't be able to keep your mind on the job," argued the manageress. "I know, I have children of my own. I can't bring them to work without going crazy."

I took courage from the fact that one of the women who worked at the bar was mooning over Kevin. Fortunately he was lapping it up and was being totally adorable.

"Look," I said. "It didn't say anywhere in the contract I signed that I couldn't bring my child to work. We live in a new South Africa. You can't discriminate against me because I'm a single parent.

He'll be fine, really. Just give us a chance. If it doesn't work out, that's OK. Please, let's see how it goes."

"Yeah," chipped in Rudd. "In fact, Kevin here, he's part of the show. He does cabaret. A real crowd puller."

The manageress laughed and shook her head. "This is madness," she said. "But I feel sorry for you. It's OK for tonight. By tomorrow night you must've made other arrangements."

One step at a time, I thought. That's how you do it climbing a rock-face. She's given me one day. We can always stretch that.

I made a bed for Kevin in a nook behind where I was sitting. Then I prayed to his guardian angel to clobber him hard over the back of the head.

"It's bedtime, Kevin," I said. "Time to go do-do."

I gave him his teddy and dummy and covered him up. He stared at me, astonished and sat up again.

"What da?" he asked, pointing to the fan revolving on the ceiling.

Oh, no, I thought. There's too much going on. He's too distracted. This isn't going to work.

"Let me take him."

The woman who helped at the bar was at my elbow. She was short, with a mischievous face and a gap between her front teeth.

"It's not busy yet. I'll get him to sleep. Why don't you sing? Maybe that'll help him doze off."

I remembered the trip to Knysna, how Kevin had sung with us all through the night.

"Maybe," I said. "Thanks . . ."

"Lindiwe."

"Thanks, Lindiwe. I'm David."

I handed Kev to her, got comfortable on the stool and tuned up. Kevin was already jigging in her arms at the mere sight of the guitar. "More!" he yelled. "More!" So I sang the Dummy Blues for him. The bar grew quieter as the few people in the place stopped talking to listen to the words. I got a couple of laughs and applause at the end.

"That was written for my son, Kevin," I told them. "He's the best thing that's ever happened to me." More applause, particularly as Kevin was clapping his hands at the idea too. Then I did a few of Just Jinger's songs, followed by Alanis Morrisette and Eric Clapton.

The pub was starting to fill up and I glanced anxiously round for Lindiwe. She'd be needed at the tables soon. I didn't want her to get into trouble. After a couple more songs, I took my first break and went to rescue her.

"C'mon, Kev," I said. "I'm going to eat some supper, then you have to go to sleep or I'm going to have to sit on you."

I couldn't believe a baby could keep going so long. I fed him some of my sausage and mash, hoping that a full tummy would swing things. It didn't. I felt an ulcer start up.

"Look, Kev," I said. "I have to work now. You have to go to sleep. Get it?"

The pub was quite full by then. Mike at the bar was eyeing me. I stuck Kev back in his little bed. He laughed like hell and got out of it again. I pulled out the baby harness, strapped it to his torso and tied the reins to a table leg.

"Now lie down!" I ordered, feeling desperate. "You'll make me lose my job." His face crumpled, his mouth opened and out came a loud wail.

"Give him here." A voice behind me. Anthony. He untied Kevin and took him in his arms. Kevin stopped wailing immediately, started tugging at Anthony's beard. I stared at him.

"So?" he said. "Are you going to play or aren't you?"

"More!" agreed Kevin with a little sob.

So I gave them more. I played fit to bust. Anthony stayed for a while, with Kevin jigging in his arms. They were my biggest fans. All in all, Kev got more attention from the crowd than I did. But it was OK. Anthony stood across the room with my baby in his arms. It was OK. The next time I looked, they'd gone.

"You play well," said Mike, as I packed up to go around twelve. "Don't worry about people talking and not listening much. They're always like that. The most of them, they treat music like background, they're more interested in the sound of their own voices."

I was grateful for that. Rudd was also coming off duty, so he gave me a lift up the hill.

"Today Knysna, tomorrow Tinseltown," he said. "I particularly liked your rendering of 'He ain't heavy, he's my brother'. I can't believe your father hasn't put two and two together. Low IQ obviously runs in the family."

"Rudd, if you let on to Anthony, I'll spread the rumour in town that you're infested with a range of genital ailments," I warned.

He hammed alarm. "My lips are sealed," he said.

There was a light on in Anthony's house when I got home. I still had the key, so I let myself in. Anthony and Kevin were snuggled up on the sofa together, fast asleep. I stood for a moment, watching them. That's what I wanted, I thought. That's what I should've had. Gently I took Kevin out of Anthony's arms. Neither of them even stirred. I left Anthony on the sofa and took Kevin upstairs.

Fifteen

Lunch time the next day I was due to play again. I'd phoned Lynne to let her and Nompumelelo know that I was going to stay in town. I'd just said, "My plans changed." So on my way to the hotel, I went to Lynne and Jill's place to drop Kevin off. My legs felt weak at the thought of seeing her again, at the thought of the fool I'd made of myself.

Lynne was busy with a customer, so I went through to the house and found Jill and Tamsyn and Nompumelelo in the kitchen.

"Hallo, little Mischief!" said Nompumelelo, sweeping Kevin out of my arms and throwing him into the air. He shrieked with delight, then seemed quite content to sit on her lap and play with some ratchet toy.

"You found someone to do nights?" asked Jill. Her tone was quite friendly, but there was something in her eyes that was cool, too cool. It made me feel uncomfortable.

"Yeah," I said. "Anthony came to the rescue."

"Anthony?" She was puzzled. She didn't know him. Relief washed through me.

"My father. The guy who was here the other day. With a beard."

"Oh, yeah. Him. He's your father?"

I nodded. They couldn't be involved with each other then.

"How do you and your ma . . . I mean, how do they know each other?"

She gesticulated around the kitchen. "He's giving Mum a quote. New kitchen cupboards."

I wanted to burst out laughing. I'd broken my very first rule in life. Explorers check things out, everything, from handholds to equipment. They measure time and distance, even their own pace. They never assume anything. Kitchen cupboards! I would never've guessed.

Lynne walked in. I looked at her with new eyes. She came over and put her arm around me. I nearly died. "It all worked out for you, then?" Her face close to mine, the pressure of her hand on my shoulder.

"You told Anthony," I said, too gently to be accusing.

She smiled. "He asked. D'you have time for some lunch before you go to work? We were just going to have something."

"Next time," I said. "I've got to go."

The lunch-time crowd were slightly more appreciative than the crowd the previous night, maybe because they were sitting down to eat, maybe because they weren't as drunk. Possibly even because I wasn't quite as nervous. I got some requests that I managed to play reasonably well and got quite a bit of applause. Rudd, as usual, had some comment to make.

"You've got to have more stage presence," he said during my break. "Throw in a couple of jokes, tell them about the meaning of life."

"When I need you to be my manager, I'll ask," I said. I knew he had a point. The music was just half the job. The performer's presence counted just as much.

"It's like being a doctor," continued Rudd, undaunted. "You may be the most technically brilliant medic in the world but without the correct bedside manner, you'll lose customers."

"Yeah. Well, I promise to hold your hand while I'm carving you into little pieces. Anyway, far be it from me to steal the whole show. Why don't you come and do a couple of jokes every now and then? Come on, admit it, you're dying to get your hands on that mike."

He raised an eyebrow. "That's a thought. I'm sure my Elvis impersonation would liven things up a bit."

I shook my head. "Uh-uh. Get this straight, Rudd. This is lunch. We don't want the customers throwing up, now do we?"

After the break, I played a couple of songs, then,

seeing that Rudd wasn't too busy at the tables, I announced, "Ladies and gentlemen, let me introduce to you my handlanger, my sidekick and general dogsbody, my *alter ego* and bank manager, Rudd Williams!"

Rudd tried to smooth his springy hair back, sauntered up to the podium and grabbed the mike. "I am obliged, ladies and gentlemen, on behalf of the management of this hotel, to warn you that listening to David here is dangerous to your mental health. I've been listening to him all my life and look what happened to me. And, as his bank manager, I must inform you that although David has quite a collection of musical notes saved in the wonderful repository of his brain, he has alarmingly few monetary notes saved in his account. So please feel free to throw bucks at him whenever he murders your favourite song or shatters your glass. Anyone who manages to hit him on the nose wins a free beer."

I groaned inwardly. I should've known Rudd would get out of control in front of an audience. To my surprise, they were laughing. And he was loving it. It must be his face, I thought.

"What," he asked to the lunchers in general, "is the difference between an orthopaedic surgeon and a rhinoceros?" He looked expectantly around the silent crowd. "The one has a very thick skin and charges a lot and the other is the rhinoceros." I hoped that there weren't any orthopaedic surgeons in the audience, also that Rudd wouldn't get too rude, or racist. I appealed with my eyes at Mike for help but he was laughing too.

After a few more, he had the grace to hand the mike back to me. "I've got them going," he said. "Don't blow it." And then he was hit on the back of the head by a five rand coin.

"What's it like working for your mother?" Jill was minding the shop when I came from work.

She shrugged. "It's a job." She wasn't giving me any gaps, although she wasn't exactly being hostile.

"I worked for my mother one holiday," I persisted. "It was a disaster. She had to get her filing system organised, which took me ages, it was such a mess. She blamed me for everything that was missing. I think that's why she employed me in the first place. She needed someone to yell at."

Jill smiled. "Yeah. Well, Mum doesn't shout at me. I'm the one who shouts."

"Maybe you could teach me. Sometimes I wish I could yell at my ma." I was making some headway. I could see her warming.

"It doesn't necessarily help. I always feel it's Lynne who's won after I've 'thrown a tantrum', as she calls it."

"What d'you yell about?"

Jill considered my face as though wondering whether to get into this at all.

"She acts so superior. She thinks she knows everything about everything. And she doesn't act her age."

This information surprised me. "You mean she doesn't sit out on the patio in a rocking chair knitting socks?" I wondered how old she was, how much age mattered.

Jill looked irritated. I shouldn't've said that.

"Of course not! But she's always wearing tight jeans and stuff. I mean, she's not exactly adolescent any more. So she shouldn't act like one. And there's all that sex stuff she gets into in her work. It's embarrassing."

Personally, I wished there were more adults around who were like Lynne, but I wasn't going to say that.

"In some ways she's OK. I suppose part of the problem is we live so on top of each other. I mean, we live together and work together. I just want more space."

"So why don't you take it?"

"Because . . . it's not easy. Not with Tamsyn. If I didn't have her, so many other things would be possible."

"Like what?"

She looked still more irritated. This was the wrong track.

"There would be more choices. Surely you know. You've got a kid yourself."

"Sure, but Kevin fits in. He's not a problem."

She had a point but I didn't want to admit it, not even to myself. I didn't ever want to resent Kevin or to give up adventure. It was just on hold for the moment, that's all. I wanted to challenge Jill, to make her see anything was possible, that she mustn't give up.

"You could change things if you wanted to. You don't have to work for your mother, or live with her, for that matter."

I'd just put my other foot in it.

"Look," said Jill curtly, "When I need your advice, I'll ask for it."

Brother, I thought, as I walked with Kevin to Anthony's place. What on earth happened there?

I told Rudd about it.

"Every time I open my mouth, something comes out that rubs her up the wrong way," I complained. "It's as though I can't do anything right."

"Why are you trying so hard with this chick?" Rudd wanted to know. "What's so special about her?"

To be honest, I didn't know. I just had the feeling

she had the wrong impression about me, that I wanted to show her the real me, one she could like. Besides, if I really fell out with Jill, that could be the end of the babysitting option. And there was something about that household that I wanted, something that attracted me, that made me want to come back for more.

"Maybe you're just a sucker for punishment," said Rudd.

I didn't like that suggestion.

"Or maybe she's just sick of the male of the species. I mean, someone must have put her up the spout and there's no sign of him around. Tell you what. Introduce her to me and I'll soon restore her faith in men."

"Thanks, buddy."

Rudd was beginning to get on my nerves.

I know what, I thought, on my way to the shop the next day. I'll say sorry. Maybe I presumed too much. I don't even know her story.

Lynne greeted me warmly as I entered the shop.

"Look what I made last night," she said and showed me a row of phallic salt and pepper pots and an equally phallic container designed to hold toothpicks.

Looking at the last one, I wondered whether there might be a sadistic streak in her.

"That one looks very uncomfortable," I pointed out.

She laughed. "Sexuality can be a thorny issue at times."

I looked at her lovely face and wanted to ask her, how do you get past the thorns, how do you get to the warmth and pleasure? Why wasn't there a man in her life? It was true what Jill'd said, her mother was wearing tight jeans; she looked stunning.

"They're amazing," I said. "What will you think of next?"

"A phallic toothbrush stand. That's what I'll be working on tonight."

With a rush I heard what she was saying. She would be here, tonight, when I finished work. Do you need a model, I wanted to ask. They're not all the same, you know. Mine might have just the contours you're looking for.

Suddenly I knew I would never be able to look at a toothbrush again as an ordinary object. That's what she's doing, I thought. She's turning the whole world into a celebration of the erotic.

I had to get out of there. I had to find Jill. She would be like a cold shower, she would bring me back to my senses.

I found her in the courtyard, playing with Tamsyn in a sandpit.

"Hi."

I plonked Kevin down next to Tamsyn. He promptly began to eat their sandcastle. Tamsyn began to wail and clunked him over the head with a plastic spade. After much comforting, we dusted them off and distracted them inside with some toys. It was early still, I wasn't in a rush to get to work. I was hoping for some tea and for a chance to make up for the previous day.

"They get on about as well as we do," I observed.

I've done it again, I saw with dismay as Jill's face hardened. But then she laughed.

"I suppose you're right," she said. "Look, I'm sorry. I was in a bad mood yesterday and what you said didn't help."

"I'm sorry too. I don't know anything about you or your circumstances. I had no right to tell you what to do."

"It's just when you said that stuff about me changing my life you sounded exactly like my mother, as though it's so easy. You sounded so superior."

That was a surprise. "I didn't mean it. Come to think of it, I could probably do with a bit of advice from you. I mean, I haven't been doing the single parent bit for very long and to tell the truth, I'm taking a bit of strain."

Jill looked interested. I'm on the right track, I thought. Slowly, now.

"What's the problem?" she asked.

"Kevin used to sleep the night through before, I never had any problems. Now he's waking up every two to three hours. I'm a walking wreck. I'm on the verge of child abuse. If he doesn't get back into sleeping through again soon, I don't know what I'll do."

Jill smiled with what looked like satisfaction.

"Ten to one, he's teething. Rub some of this on his gums at night before he goes to sleep and also if he wakes at night."

She scratched in a drawer and handed me a tube of gel.

"If that doesn't help, you should take him to the doctor to get his ears checked. If there's nothing wrong with his ears and it's not his teeth, then welcome to the real world."

She smiled at me encouragingly. She could be an ally I thought, looking at the tube. I had found a way through.

"Thanks," I said. "Why didn't I think of asking you about this earlier?"

Sixteen

"So how's your sex life?" Rudd wanted to know. We were grabbing something to eat in the hotel kitchen late that night after work.

"Very safe," I retorted. "So safe I don't even need condoms."

"Why? You haven't figured out how to get to the underbelly of old Prickly Pear?"

I wasn't mad about Rudd calling Jill a prickly pear.

"Actually, things are going better. We're swapping baby notes. She's donated me a supply of teething gel which'll change my life."

He looked at me like I was off my head. "You call that progress? Now, if she'd given you a tube of lubricant, I'd call that progress."

"You know, Rudd, there's more to life than sex."

"Jeez, are you in trouble. You're starting to sound like Mrs Blundell."

I narrowed my eyes. "And you? You making headway?"

He shook his head. "It's very unfair. Humans are

teeming with sex hormones and raring to go from the age of thirteen, but the objects of our desire get turned off by the side-effects of that very condition." He pointed to a new chorb erupting volcanically on his chin.

"Yeah," I said, dreaming of Jill, dreaming of Lynne.

"It's like we're living life in the wrong gear. When you're young your hormones want to drive at top speed, but society's fixed it that the handbrake's always on. Then when you're married and can go all out it seems men are more interested in the sports channel on TV."

"You think so?" That sounded like Trevor, like the men I didn't want to be.

"They say interest in sex dies off after a couple of years of marriage. All these ripe years wasted. All those lovely chicks out there and I can't get my hands on them."

I glanced at him sideways. "Y'know, maybe Mrs Blundell was right, to a point. Maybe girls look for something more in a man than eager hands."

Rudd smacked his hand to his brow in mock revelation. "Hell, I wonder what else they might be looking for?"

I sighed. I hadn't worked that one out either.

"You guys still here?" Lindiwe put her head in at the swing door.

"Yeah," said Rudd, brightening. "We're trying to work out what chicks desire in a man."

Lindiwe came over and helped herself to some cheese and biscuits. "Oh, I can't tell you that," she said. "That's half the attraction."

"Come on!" urged Rudd, his blood up. "If you tell me, I'll let you in on what men look for in chicks."

Lindiwe pulled a face. "I know that already," she said. "You guys are so transparent. That's part of the problem."

"To think the nation is calling out for government to be more transparent! Some people would regard transparency as a virtue!"

Lindiwe licked her fingers. "There's a difference between transparency and being skin deep."

Rudd rolled his eyes. "You really know how to make a guy's day," he said.

"You asked for it. Expecting a girl to make a guy's day is just one aspect of being skin-deep." She turned and left, saying as she went, "Cheers, guys. See you tomorrow."

Rudd looked at me in despair. "Did I say something wrong?" he asked.

I nodded. "Plenty. The consolation is that all you need to grow a crop of magnificent chorbs is skin. And we males, we got plenty of that."

*

The streets were practically empty by the time Rudd and I staggered out of the hotel, despite it being a Friday night. It's late, I thought. She won't be up now. I'd been procrastinating, passing the time talking bull with Rudd, trying to put off a decision that was gnawing a hole in my brain.

"I'll give you a lift, eh?"

I shook my head. "No, thanks, buddy. I feel like a walk."

"Suit yourself. See you tomorrow."

I started off, not up the hill, but along the main road. I'd just go past, I'd just go and see whether there was a light on. There was. Now what? Now I wanted to enter, to be enveloped in warmth, to be welcomed in.

I was drunk. This was mad. My eyes were heavy with tiredness but I didn't want to go on up the hill to Anthony's house, to Kev waking all the time, wanting me, more and more of me. I wanted to sit quietly for a while, watching her work, drinking her tea. Nourished by her words and glances. I felt terrified, stupid, crazy.

Up the hill, the cold house of my father. Here before me a warm house, a woman's house, a home where I could belong. I thought of all the many houses and flats I'd lived in as a child, rented, ugly places, places that mostly belonged to the men in my mother's life. None of them a home, not like my gran's place, not like this.

I don't know how long I stood there on the pavement, it felt like ages, it started to get really cold. No, this was how it'd always been, ever since my gran died. I was on my own, the coldness kept me awake, it kept my life together. If I got too warm, I would relax and my life would fall apart. Or, if the warm got warmer, it'd become hot water. For Kevin's sake I couldn't do something stupid, I had to keep my head. I turned away and took the next road up the hill.

"Where the hell have you been?" Anthony glared at me from the sofa.

"Da!" exclaimed Kevin with glee. The paste for the gums. I'd forgotten to tell Anthony about the paste.

"Oh, what time is it?"

"Half past three! Y'know, I have to work in the morning! I'll remind you I'm doing you a favour here looking after Kev, but it's so you can earn some bucks! How can you take advantage of me like this!"

I glared back. Who did he think I was that he thought he could yell at me like this? Besides, it was the least he could do. I never had a break, not like him. He could give me one little break, couldn't he? He knew there was more to life than working and looking after babies!

"I didn't know it was so late. Anyway, I wasn't jolling. Rudd and I had some business to discuss." My head was spinning, I needed to put it down on something soft.

"Don't give me that bullshit!"

"Look, if doing me a favour is too much to ask you, then I'll make another arrangement. If you don't care about Kev and me, don't bother."

"That's not the point, David. The point is that *my* shift here with Kev ends a quarter of an hour after *your* shift at the hotel ends."

I glowered at him. What was he in such a hurry for, anyway? I lifted Kevin and took him upstairs. I also had a life to live, selfish bastard. I shouldn't have come back, I should've stayed with Lynne. I didn't need this.

The next morning, I woke up steeped in regret. I'd had two hours' sleep, but Kevin didn't care.

"Uppie!" he pleaded, trying to get at the door-knob to open the door. "Uppie!"

I'd used the whole tube of gel on his gums during the night, thinking that either he'd get some relief, or he would pass out from a gel overdose, but nothing had induced him to go back to sleep for a couple of hours. This wasn't fair. I pictured Tracey having a good lie-in with her latest and wanted to kill her. I'll phone home today and find out where she is. I'll get her to come and fetch Kev immediately.

"Uppie!" wailed Kev.

"Shut up!" I yelled at him. It worked for about one second while he recovered from the shock, then he cried even harder.

What the hell did I think I was doing last night, mooning around at the hotel with Rudd until all hours, then pacing the pavements like some love-struck fool? I'd been behaving as though I was free, as though I didn't have this ball and chain around my neck, as though I had real parents who would help out.

After a while I gave up, took a cold shower and bought some Lert tablets on the way down to the shop.

"Nompumelelo," I begged. "I'll pay you anything this afternoon if you look after Kevin so I can get some sleep."

She shook her head. "Sorry, David. I have to visit the school. Maybe tomorrow?" Tomorrow was twenty-four hours away. I would be dead by then.

"Didn't that gel help?" asked Jill.

"Yeah, it did at first, but I forgot to tell Anthony about it and by the time I got home, it was late and he'd been up for hours with Kev. Then it took a while to get him to sleep and the next thing the sun came up. Kev always wakes up when the sun comes up. It triggers his inner alarm, or something."

"You out on the tiles last night?"

"Not exactly. Rudd and me were being dissected by some chick who works at the hotel."

I felt Jill stiffen. What'd I done now?

"She reckons that men are skin deep. Luckily my skin is deep enough to protect me from such an attack."

"You really know how to get up my nose, don't you?"

"What? What did I do?"

"That stuff about chicks, it really gets to me."

"Why? It doesn't mean anything!"

"Of course it does! It means exactly what it says! That you regard women as fluffy and ineffectual, as unintelligent and powerless!"

Oh, hell. She was picking on me, she overreacted to anything I did or said.

"Well, I'm sorry," I said defensively. "That's not what I meant." I thought of Tracey, of Lynne. I thought of my gran and of Beverley. And of Jill, still cross in front of me. None of them were exactly chick-like. I hadn't meant that at all. "If someone called me a rooster, I don't think it'd upset me."

Her face darkened still further. Why didn't I just shut up.

"That's the point! Roosters are not associated with powerlessness and insignificance! Of *course* you wouldn't mind."

I supposed she had a point there. I hadn't exactly thought about it that way. On the other hand, I didn't want to have to watch every word I said in front of Jill. Maybe this was too much effort. Maybe all my childcare arrangements would fall through in one go.

"I think my skin just gave in," I said, collapsing with a groan on to the ground and clutching at my heart. Jill, Tamsyn and Kevin stared at me in astonishment, then Jill burst out laughing and Kev toddled over with glee and sat on my head.

"Good," she said. "Then there's hope."

"Hope for what?"

"Hope that there's something beneath that hide of yours. A certain sensitivity. Compassion even?"

Passion? Did someone say something about passion?

"Yeah," I said, somewhat muffled by Kevin's nappy. "I can just feel it bubbling out of the dent in my armour. Passionate compassion. Rations of fashionable passion."

Consider that an invitation. Do to me what you will, you Amazon Conqueror. But Jill just laughed as Tamsyn tried to join in the fun and stood heavily on my groin.

"Right," I groaned, rolling around in semi-agony. "Tamsyn's stamped out any possibility of that."

"Are you OK?"

"Well, my prospects are ruined, but other than

that I'm fine." I proceeded to lay it on thick and got a bit of compassion in return, a cup of tea and some milk tart. *And* Jill offered to look after Kevin for the afternoon. I didn't even get to finish my tea, but passed out on the sofa with a cushion over my head and slept like a baby. At least, I slept like a baby ought to sleep. I don't know how any parent of a small child copes without back-up.

So thanks to Jill, when I went to work that evening I was functional and feeling better than I had in a long while. It's amazing how sleep deprivation colours one's view of the world. I even felt magnanimous enough to apologise to Anthony. A part of me knew that I hadn't exactly been fair on him. But now there could be no more late-night rendezvous in the kitchen or the shop.

That thought depressed me momentarily, but my mood revived when Jill phoned to invite Kev and me to go on a picnic with the three of them the following day, my day off. I accepted eagerly. It was something to look forward to, something that felt like progress on to the next stepping-stone of my life.

Seventeen

Anthony, Kev and I sat down to a breakfast of eggs and toast the next morning and looked at each other blearily.

"When you offered me the job of devoted nocturnal grandfather, you promised me this child slept through," he said, but in a friendly kind of way. The gel hadn't helped, but the apology had.

"Don't remind me," I said. "Now I know why everyone always told me I was lucky to have such an easy baby." I tapped Kev on his shoulder to divert his attention from the mess of egg on his plate. "You're slipping," I admonished him. "You're becoming average." He beamed at me happily and threw his spoon on to the floor for the four thousand and sixty-second time.

"Gone," he informed me proudly. "All gone."

"He's the only one who's anywhere near awake around here," complained Anthony.

"Tinkle, tinkle, tinkle, tinkle," sang Kevin, rocking in his high chair.

"I'm going sailing today," said Anthony. "If you

organise some child care, you're welcome to come along."

I shook my head. "No, thanks. I'm going round to Lynne's."

"Quite a nice daughter she's got there."

I shrugged. I wasn't about to discuss girls with Anthony. I wondered who he was going sailing with. I'd only met two of his friends, both male and Vossie, the guy who worked with him.

"Actually, it's for Kevin's sake. He's really into Tamsyn. Or maybe it's only her toys. Whaddya say, Kev?"

Kev threw his spoon on to the floor again. "All gone!" he beamed.

"This is worse than having a dog," said Anthony, picking it up and putting it out of Kevin's reach. Kevin started to wail. "Poon!" he sobbed, reaching across the table towards it. "Poon!" Anthony gave it back to him. He beamed victoriously and threw it on to the floor. Anthony pulled Kevin out of the high chair and put him on the floor too. "Now go fetch!" he ordered. "Go fetch it yourself!"

"Kids teach you patience," I commented. "Amongst other things."

"Yeah," he said. "I can believe it." He watched Kevin lurching after the cat. "He's so much like you were," he said.

"I'll take that as a compliment."

"Sure. You were a great kid." He fiddled with his beard and looked out of the window. "We knew so little then, Tracey and me. It's so weird, how you have kids when you aren't old enough to know how to do it better, while your relationship with your partner is still so new and there's so much to work out. On top of it there's a little creature you have to nurture and cherish and provide for. You still feel like a kid yourself in many ways." He looked at me. "At least, that's how it was for me."

This was interesting, I wanted to hear him talk more about himself, about him and me.

Anthony said, "How's Tracey?"

I shrugged. "Dunno. OK."

"She still with that guy, what's his name?"

"Trevor. No. I don't think so."

He raised his eyebrows. "I wonder whether she'll ever find what she's looking for."

What did he mean by that? He was acting the great psychologist, as though what happened had nothing to do with him.

"Have you?"

"What?"

"Found what you've been looking for?"

He shrugged. "In a way."

How's your sex life, I wanted to ask. Tell me

about your life, show me something of yourself. I can't trust you while you're so hidden.

Anthony was still staring at me intently. It made me uncomfortable. "She didn't do too badly in the end," he said.

"What d'you mean?"

"I was worried for years that Tracey'd stuff you up, you know. But she must've done something right. You're OK."

I felt a churn of feeling, a heat where it was usually cold. A strange mix, like embarrassment, anger and pleasure all rolled into one. I stood up.

"Yeah. Well. I'd better be going." I dragged Kevin out, protesting, from under the sofa where he'd been molesting the cat, and went to the door. I stopped, feeling the distance between myself and my father. It was better that way.

"Have a nice day," I said. I went out of the door.

Lynne, Jill and Tamsyn were waiting when we arrived. Jill seemed to be in a better mood. I couldn't fathom her, she seemed to blow from hot to cold and back again with no warning and no particular reason. We got into their combi and headed out of town.

"Where're we going?" I wanted to know.

"It's a secret," said Lynne, who was sitting in the

back with me and the babies. "We have to blindfold initiates." She took a scarf out of her basket and tied it over my eyes. I had a sudden vision of the two of them ravishing me in a secluded part of the forest somewhere, still with the blindfold on and nearly passed out at the thought of it.

"You two aren't man-haters, by any chance," I said, as soon as I'd got my voice back. "If I'm found on a deserted beach with a knife in my back, they'll be able to trace you, you know."

"No point!" said Jill. "There are too many more where you come from. Only when there's genetic engineering and artificial insemination on a large enough scale can we rid the earth of men!"

"Oh. I must say I've never considered myself redundant before. It's a new thought."

"Actually, you're far from redundant at present. We've brought you along to mind the kids, carry the picnic, make the sandwiches and clean up afterwards, haven't we, Mum?"

"Amongst other things."

The combi bumped along on what felt like a dirt road. This was somewhere I hadn't been before, that was certain. I could feel Kevin straining on my lap to dislodge the blindfold. He thought this was a game of peek-a-boo. He didn't understand yet that adults have games of their own.

"No, you don't." I felt Lynne whip him off my lap. "You sit here with me."

After about half an hour we came to a halt.

"OK," said Jill. "You can take it off now."

We were parked at the verge of a forest. Where the dirt track stopped, a path began, disappearing between the trees. We loaded up and started out. It was so peaceful, with the soft moulding leaves underfoot, the birds calling to each other in the branches. Until the kids started up. Then it sounded as though the circus was coming to town.

The path carried on through the forest for a way, then started to dip down towards the sound of running water. I'd been told to bring a costume and towel, so this wasn't unexpected. The path stopped at the edge of a bouldered river that lazed through a small kloof. Upstream, the kloof got narrower and the river was bounded by cliffs overhung with indigenous vegetation.

"This is where we swim," said Lynne, stripping down to her costume. They put my clobber into a refuse bag and tied it tightly at the neck, then rammed it into a rucksack, similarly prepared.

They'd brought Bentley belts for the babies and they were launched into the dark water with much shrieking and squealing. I was grateful that Kev had been initiated into water adventures at the Newlands swimming pool – he took to this like a dream.

The three of us swam leisurely upstream through the kloof, pushing the floating babies and rucksacks ahead of us. Tamsyn and Kevin discovered there was an echo in the kloof and ruined the occasion from an auditory point of view. Water dripped from an overhang on to our heads at one point, which amplified their shrieks.

"This place is called Dripkelder," explained Lynne. "Not many people know about it and we want to keep it that way."

"Cross my heart and hope to die," I said. Wait till Rudd hears I'm one of the chosen few, I thought, nearly drowning with pleasure.

We emerged on the other side of the kloof to beach ourselves on to boulders, baking dry in the warm sun. There was one flat enough and large enough to contain the babies and together with the diversion of food and each of us taking it in turns to be vigilant, they survived the day with only one bumped head and one near-drowning.

"This is the life," I murmured, close to sleep during one of my off-duty patches. Jill was on baby guard, Lynne was lying near me.

I felt lucky, as though I had my guardian angel back. But how lucky, I wondered. Lucky enough to take a risk with Lynne? The thought caught in my gut making me aware of the rock pressing hard into my back. She was out of my league, it would be ridiculous.

Yet I was aware of some thin wire of desire snapping between us all the time. It had to be imagined, right? The wire was only attached my end, the only snapping was in my head. I sneaked a glance in her direction and found her looking at me.

"Pity we couldn't bring the guitar," she said. "You owe me a lesson."

"Sure. Any time. Pity there's no clay out here either."

She smiled.

"How d'you decide what you want to make? I mean, what inspires you?"

She thought for a moment. "Well, there's two ways, no, three, that I go about making things. One is to keep up with the general stock in the shop, stuff tourists go for. That keeps the wolf from the door. Then there's commissioned work, some of which is thematic, like the erotica exhibition in Jo'burg, or prescribed in some other way by the client. Then there are works that come in their entirety from the inside. They're what I like to do best. But they don't sell particularly well in Knysna. You just have to look around in the wood and curio shops to see what kind of kitsch sells."

"Where do you even start? I mean, how do you find out what's on the inside?"

She considered this. "Sometimes I start with a dream image. Just a shape. But once you've started, you can't predict where it's going. You just have to follow what's happening. Often, mistakes can be doors into something new and unexpected." She smiled. "It's taken me most of my life to learn to trust my mistakes."

I wanted to believe her. I wanted to forgive myself the mistakes I'd made.

She was quiet for a moment, deep in thought. Then she said, "If you want to be really creative, you have to break rules sometimes."

I'd never heard this from a parent before! I thought of Trevor, strapped under the bonnet of a car, strapped to his bottle, dishing out rules. I thought of astronauts, rocketing into space where ordinary rules like gravity don't apply.

"You mean, like anarchy?"

"What I mean is, sometimes you have to break limits in order to grow."

"Like explorers?" She wasn't treating me like a kid, like most parents. I wanted more.

"Well, yeah. True artists are explorers. Tchaikovsky for example."

"Yeah, what a great painter. "

Lynne tried unsuccessfully to suppress a smile. "Tchaikovsky's a composer who lived in the nineteenth century."

The world shrank; I wanted to crawl under the boulder.

"Who knows, maybe he was a painter on the side!" She didn't have to do this, try to salvage my pride. "Talking about painters, Picasso is another example."

"Yeah?" I faltered. "Right, Picasso. So what rules did they break?"

"They took incredible risks, painting and composing in ways foreign to their cultures. At the time they were ridiculed but it didn't stop them. Afterwards people were able to see what extra-ordinary works they'd created. If those geniuses had stuck to what was known and acceptable, they wouldn't have pioneered those breakthroughs in ways of seeing and hearing and feeling. They broke the rules of society in such a way that society itself had to change."

Pioneers; pioneers of the spirit. I wanted to be like that, I wanted her to keep talking. But she turned to Jill.

"Time for lunch, I do believe. Even potential geniuses like ourselves have to eat."

I sprang to my feet. "That's my cue, I think." I wanted to be invited again, I wanted to prove to Jill I wasn't some male chauve.

They'd brought a feast of olive bread and

camembert, aubergine pâté and hoummus. We sipped red wine and ate our fill. Kevin spat the aubergine pâté out in disgust.

"Dry bread for you, then, buddy," I said, handing him a rusk. He threw it into the water and watched it float downstream with fascination.

"No, Kevin!" I said sternly. "Now it's all gone!"

Kevin's face crumpled as the rusk disappeared around a bend in the river. "More!" he appealed, stretching his chubby little hand in the direction the rusk had disappeared. "More!" he wailed.

Suddenly I saw what he was doing, with the spoon, with the rusk. He was playing with the idea that objects and people in his life come and go, that they aren't constant. Things disappear, but if they return, nothing is lost. When he played this game, or peek-a-boo, he was trying to be in control of the process of loss and return, to understand better how it worked.

I dived into the water and swam downstream. When I gave what was left of the soggy, disintegrating rusk back to him, his face lit up with pleasure. The rusk hadn't disappeared off the edge of the earth, it was restored to him.

"Now don't you do that again," I warned him. But he had other plans. He'd turned his attention to applying the pasty rusk to the rock as an art work.

"You're really patient with him," said Jill.

I felt my ears heat up. I thought of all the times I'd screamed at him when he was being impossible.

"Sometimes. I guess I try to see things from his point of view. Plus, I had a rough time as a baby. I want things better for him than they were for me."

"Does he miss his mother much? I mean, does he remember her at all, d'you think?"

Good question. Then again, I'd done more mothering of Kevin than Tracey had. But that wasn't what she meant.

"Yeah. I mean, I don't know." Then I remembered what I'd said to Lynne. "I mean, he can't really. He was taken out of her belly as she lay dying."

Something squirmed in me every time I lied to these women.

"How awful." Jill looked pensive. "It's such a strange thought to me, that if I died, Tamsyn'd have no memory of me at all as she grew up."

I couldn't stand it. I didn't want subterfuge any more.

"Look. You've let me into a wonderful secret today. I want to let you into one of mine, OK?" They looked at me, interested. "But don't tell anyone. Especially Anthony."

"Sure," said Jill. Lynne nodded. Could I trust them? It was too late now.

"I'm not Kevin's father. I'm his brother. His half-brother."

"Oh," said Jill, astonished.

Lynne stared at me, then to my annoyance, she burst out laughing.

"Sorry," she said, noticing my face. "It's just that . . . Well, here I am, talking about rule-breaking and you're already doing brilliantly!" I didn't know what she was talking about. "I mean, you're young. Young to be a father and doing better at it than most men I know, young and old. You relate really well to Kevin, you're on his wavelength. But you're not even his father! You're a young and single man! Yet you've taken this baby on as your own. I've never even heard of that before!"

I felt confused and embarrassed and pleased. She was complimenting me, but I wasn't so keen on her referring all the time to how young I was. Suddenly I could see myself in her eyes, some pimply, gawky adolescent. I was crazy to consider that she might take me seriously.

"Why is it a secret?" Jill wanted to know. "Where are Kevin's parents?"

I couldn't tell them the truth without explaining it. So I began at the beginning, at Kevin's birth and told them everything. They sat riveted and engrossed and it was a relief to tell them, to talk about things I hadn't mentioned to anyone else, the anger, the hurt. They were so focused on my story, that child care was briefly forgotten. That's when we had the near-drowning, but once Tamsyn had stopped choking and wailing, both kids had a nap and I was able to continue with the next episode. By the end, I could see admiration shining in their eyes.

"I still don't understand why it's a secret," said Jill.

"Anthony and Tracey hate each other. If he knew that Kevin was Tracey's child, he wouldn't help me out. He might even report her to the child welfare. Kevin might be taken away into foster care."

"We won't say a word," Jill assured me.

"We won't need to," said Lynne. "This isn't something that can keep itself a secret for very long, David. At some point your father's going to find out. Maybe it's better if it comes from you."

She was treating me like a child. "I'll take my chances," I told her coldly. Her remark had spoilt everything. She was criticising me, she was holding me responsible.

"I'm going to have a last swim," I said and plunged into the silky water.

Eighteen

"This place is a dump," said Rudd.

We were sitting on the terrace of the hotel one afternoon, having come off duty. Out on the lagoon a couple of yachts and windsurfers were flying along on a stiff breeze. It looked fun. Maybe I would go with my father next time, I thought. Maybe Rudd would look after Kevin.

"It's OK," I said. "I've been in worse places."

"Trouble is, female holiday-makers don't take waiters seriously. It must be some class thing. If you've got the money to go on holiday, you aren't interested in someone who has to work for money during the holidays."

"Something like that," I agreed.

"You seem to be doing all right." There was a barb in his voice. I hadn't been seeing much of Rudd, except at work. "How's it going with that dark-haired chick?"

I froze. Rudd was bound to meet Jill and Lynne at some point and I didn't want him stuffing up my chances.

"She's not a chick, Rudd!"

"Chick, goose, bird, it's all the same. When did you care?"

"Listen, buddy, I got my groin stood on for less. Women don't like being called names like that. It's derogatory."

He scrutinised me through his dark glasses. "Hey man, you're too serious, you know? It's just a name."

"Like Kaffir and Hotnot are just names." We glared at each other.

"That's different." Rudd's tone was suddenly cold.

"It's not. If you demean people, they're going to get mad at you. I have first-hand experience."

"I know plenty of chicks who don't mind being called chicks. I even know some who call themselves chicks."

I didn't like his point, but he had one. Then a thought came to my rescue.

"If you call someone a name for long enough, they start to think of themselves in those terms. I was called Big Ears for years at school. I had a huge complex about my ears. I used to stick them down with tape at night when I slept to try to flatten them so that they'd look smaller. Then one day I realised that they weren't *that* big. I'd just believed those stupid jerks all those years."

"Come off it, David! You *have* got big ears! Only now you hide them behind all that hair!"

He was being obnoxious. But I wasn't giving in. I felt like a knight in shining armour out to champion the cause of women. And Rudd was being a pain in the butt.

"And what about the gardener my Gran had. His parents gave him the English name of Kaffir-boy! Can you believe it! He didn't seem to mind it. We called him by his Xhosa name, Velelo."

"Y'know, David, you really are scraping the bottom of the barrel to prove your point. What for? D'you really think I treat women without respect?"

I stared back at him. "Yes. I do."

"Well, that's great, coming from you! You treat women like they're goddesses, or mothers! Y'know what, David, you're scared of women, that's what you are. That's why you have to make up these weird theories around how to treat them, how not to make them mad, how to avoid them. Check in with the real world, man! Women don't live on pedestals!"

That evening I didn't invite Rudd to the mike and he didn't come to take it. We just ignored each other and I went through a routine set. I felt depressed and upset. I was right about the name-calling and labelling, but what if Rudd was right about the other stuff? Was I really scared of women?

The following Sunday, early, I went over to Lynne's again. I'd been tempted to go sailing with Anthony, but there was the problem of child care. Rudd and I weren't getting on well enough for me to ask him and it was his only day off too. And I still felt irresistibly drawn into my cauldron of feelings around Lynne.

There was another outing planned but I didn't know that it didn't include Lynne.

"You can leave Kevin with me today," she said. "I'm already looking after Tamsyn. You'll have a nicer time without babies getting in the way." She gave the keys of the combi to Jill. "Drive carefully," she said.

My heart sank. Jill looked on top of the world.

"We're going to the old road bridge," she said, heading out of town. "Have you ever eaten fresh Knysna crab before?"

I shook my head.

"Well, last night my friends and I set traps with fish heads in them and had a party around a bonfire up there. Pity you had to work. It was such fun. Anyway, at least you're around today to share in the spoils."

Of course she didn't want her mother around. I'd started to think of the two of them as a unit.

"It was kind of your ma to take the kids," I said.

"Yeah. She's good with kids."

"Tamsyn's father's not involved?"

She shook her head. "Tamsyn's father doesn't know about Tamsyn."

I was shocked. "Why not?"

She shrugged. "It was a brief affair. And he didn't bother to ask. He doesn't even live in Knysna. Thank God. Otherwise I suppose he'd have to know."

Another secret. "That must've been hard for you."

"Ja. It was." She looked at me. "On the other hand, you got yourself a child without the fun of having sex."

I was even more shocked. She was laughing at me!

Jill giggled and turned off the main road. "You're so serious," she said. "You don't like me teasing you, do you?"

I'd never thought of myself as serious before and yet two people had told me I was in as many days.

"No," I offered. "It's fine. Tease me if you want to. Take out all your pent-up frustrations on this poor city slicker. I don't mind."

She smiled at me. "OK," she said.

We arrived at the old road bridge to find about eight bulky sleeping bags strewn around an extinct bonfire. Jill launched herself on to the sleeping forms mercilessly.

"Wake up!" she yelled. "Who's going to cook breakfast!" Six men and two women emerged, protesting, from their cocoons.

"For God's sake, Jill!" complained a tall, lanky guy. "The party carried on after you left last night. We've only just gone to bed!"

"That's not my problem! C'mon! Wake up! I'm starved."

I watched as the lanky guy made a grab for her ankle, then, when he missed, jumped out of his sleeping bag and chased her down the road. The others looked at me blearily. I shifted uncomfortably. I wished I hadn't come.

"Hi," I offered. "I'm David."

By the time the lanky guy returned with Jill slung over his shoulder screaming and flailing, the others had introduced themselves and I'd promptly forgotten their names. But I remembered the lanky guy's name. Pete. I followed him and two others and Jill on to the bridge where they hauled up the traps from the river bed. Eleven crabs in all. Big red carapaces glistening in the morning light. Scrabbly legs, pincers snapping angrily. The fire was soon going again and Pete put a large pot of water on it, quickly putting an end to their aggression.

The cooked crab meat was delicious, tender and subtly flavoured. But I felt a fraud, an outsider. I didn't even know how to relate to Jill, she seemed so changed today. More outgoing, less serious. I wondered why. Maybe she was in love with that moron Pete. Maybe because her mother wasn't around. Or Tamsyn. Maybe she felt freer without Tamsyn.

I got quieter and quieter. I thought of slipping away and walking back to town, to Lynne. I thought of my father sailing.

Jill came and sat next to me.

"You're very quiet," she said, giving me another morsel.

"Yeah."

"You OK?"

I nodded.

"You mustn't mind these guys. I grew up with them. Went to school with them." Screwed them, I thought to myself.

"Why didn't you sleep here last night? With them?"

Jill looked at me. "Tamsyn was with me. She wouldn't have got into it. She likes her own bed. And I wanted to bring you this morning." Then she laughed. "Besides, the ground is very hard."

"You seem very different today." She raised an eyebrow. "Less . . . hassled."

A frown flitted across her face. She looked into the fire, twirled a strand of hair around a finger.

"Yeah. I feel less hassled. I mean, don't you ever get the feeling . . . Don't you ever feel that you lost

out? That being responsible for a child so young, you lost out on a lot of . . . this?"

She gestured around her, at her friends, at the camp-site. "I mean, if Tamsyn was here, I couldn't just hang out. I'd have to be watching her, making sure that she didn't get hurt, or drown. I'd have to feed her, change her nappy, all that."

She had a point. Maybe that's why I felt so out of things, here, with these people. I didn't often get to be in these situations any more. But there were other factors.

"I suppose. I've always been a bit of a loner. I'm afraid that I'm not very good at social occasions. If I had my guitar now, I'd play it. It's a way of being part of what's going on, but not a part of it. I guess you could call me background music."

She smiled. "I prefer being with other people than by myself." Her face grew more serious. "Ma says things like, if you don't like your own company, you aren't good friends with yourself and if you aren't good friends with yourself, you're in trouble. It makes me mad."

Sometimes keeping your own company gets lonely, I wanted to tell to her. I suddenly felt shy.

"She's so critical of me, d'you notice? Everyone else loves her, she's so beautiful and good at what she does and kind and generous, it makes me so mad!

They don't know what a pain she can be, how undermining."

She was studying my face as she said this, she was looking for my response. I was horrified to feel my neck heating up.

"Why compare yourself to her?" I asked quickly. "You're a lovely person in your own right, only you disappear when you're with your mother. It's like you've come out from behind a cloud today, now you're not with her."

Her face had opened up, something had relaxed in it. She looked pleased by what I'd said.

"I can't be myself around my mother. I never feel good enough for anything when I'm with her. She's even better at looking after Tamsyn than I am." She looked close to tears.

"You're too hard on yourself. You know what? You're much more critical of yourself than your mother is, as far as I can make out."

She sniffed and took a hanky out of her pocket. "But it's true!" she said, blowing her nose. "When I look at you and Kevin, I can see I'm no good as a mother!" She stood up, took my hand and pulled me up from the ground. "Let's go for a walk," she said.

We walked down the road in silence for a while. I felt light-headed and confused. Suddenly I could see things from Jill's perspective. I remembered my dream. Lynne was lovely, but she'd moulded me, she'd been about to eat me. There was something too powerful about her, something I couldn't cope with. Now I was aware of Jill's body next to mine, of her breathing.

Our steps fell into a natural rhythm together. I didn't want to break the silence. It held fragile possibilities that words might fracture. I glanced at her face; it looked troubled, vulnerable. I remembered how we'd met, in the library, the day she'd looked so cross, yet I'd seen something there that had made me follow her into the arms of her life. It was something I recognised, something that looked hard from the outside but was soft and insecure on the inside.

I thought of Rudd, of his stinging words. Why was it so hard for me to reach out and touch a woman? Here was one who was in reach, who wasn't on a pedestal. You're nineteen years old, I told myself. It's time you grew up.

All you'll find there is trouble.

How do you know?

Relationships are trouble. From the outside they look soft, but on the inside they get stuck between a rock and a very hard place.

Those are Tracey's words. It doesn't have to be like that.

You're sentimental. A fool.

Well, you aren't exactly wise. In fact you're weird. What's wrong with a bit of trouble? Avoiding trouble is like avoiding life. If you avoid trouble, you'll never get to be an explorer. It's how you handle it that matters.

"A penny for your thoughts?"

With a start I realised that we had walked quite far. The river wound on to my left; on my right was a flesh and blood woman.

"Oh . . . I'm just having an argument with myself."

"About what?"

"About . . . whether or not it would be possible . . . I mean, all other things considered . . . what would happen if . . ."

"If what?"

I stopped walking, looked down. My feet were too big, that was the real problem. It wasn't sexy to have such big feet.

"If what?" Jill repeated, somewhat impatiently.

"I . . . Um . . ." How to get out of this, what to say. The sky streaked with clouds flying above me, the huge red earth under my enormous sandalled feet. Jill burst out laughing. I scowled at her.

"I was afraid you'd laugh," I said.

That stopped her. She looked at me quizzically, concerned.

Could I trust her? I wondered. Could I trust my own impulse?

I took her lovely face between my hands and kissed her.

Nineteen

"Stay for supper," Jill offered, picking Tamsyn up and giving her a hug.

It was quite late by the time we got back. I would've loved to. But there were other considerations. Always other people to consider.

"It's my night to cook." Kevin was pulling my hair, something he'd started to do recently and enjoyed precisely because it irritated me. I would have to cut it off if this carried on. He was even trying to influence how I looked. "Stop it, Kev!"

"So? Invite your father around here. We'll make some pasta," Lynne said. She was looking wonderful. Too wonderful. I didn't want Anthony seeing her like that. I didn't want to share this life with him. He would come in, take over, take it away from me. I shook my head.

"I can't. He likes to spend Sunday evenings at home. He's a kind of recluse, you know. A bit weird."

"Then swap nights with him. Let him cook for himself."

That was a thought. But I still felt unsure. If I

stuffed Anthony around too much, he might chuck me out.

"Another time. I'd love to, but Anthony's not the easiest guy." I looked at Jill. "I'll come early tomorrow."

"I went out yesterday and bought a guitar," said Lynne.

"That's a good place to start." I felt pleased. She really was keen. "I could show you some chords tomorrow. I could give you a lesson."

"I'd like that," she said. Jill was looking from me to her as she said this.

"You're too old to learn guitar, Mum!"

"Oh, rubbish!" she said irritably. "Wait until you're my age, my girl then see whether you think that sort of thing!"

"You can learn too, Jill," I offered quickly. "I can teach you both."

Jill shook her head. "Someone has to mind the shop," she said pointedly. "Besides, I'm not really interested."

There was a seam of resentment in her tone, but I chose to ignore it. You can't make someone want to do something, I reasoned with myself. I was on too much of a high to let anything spoil it. I'd taken a risk with Jill and kissed her and it'd been fine. Better than fine. I couldn't wait to tell Rudd. But on second thoughts,

I wouldn't tell him. Not yet. I'd just drop a comment casually, once it was well on the road, once I was sure it had wheels.

"I'm going to build a yacht. A twenty-six footer."

Anthony was sitting at the kitchen table opposite me, his beard stiff with salt, his face burnished by the sun. Their boat had come second in the regatta. He wiped his bowl clean with a piece of bread.

"D'you have any skills? Carpentry, or working with fibreglass?"

"I did woodwork for matric. I'm good with my hands. I can learn anything." Could it be that he wanted me to . . . what? I daren't hope.

He settled back in his chair. "I'll need help. I'd pay you. Not a fortune, but enough. More than you're earning at the moment."

I felt something leap inside me. OK! I could do that. A thought sobered me.

"I've got a contract with the hotel until the middle of January. When do you need to start?"

"Oh, not before then."

"Right. You're on."

"Are you sure? It'll be hard work."

I nodded. Sure I was sure.

Anthony smiled. "You'll be on probation for a month," he warned. "I just need to be certain that you can build this craft so that the bloody thing doesn't sink on hitting the first bit of driftwood."

It was Anthony who wasn't sure. I smiled back at him. Don't forget that you're on probation too, buddy, I thought. Don't you ever forget that. There was a small part of me that was worried about working for my father. It gave him too much power. But the job meant I didn't have to go back to Cape Town. And it was interesting. And building the means to adventure was getting closer to the real thing.

"You mean, like this?"

I nodded. I'd shown Lynne a couple of chords and started her off on that old standard, 'The House of the Rising Sun'. She had a lovely voice. All she needed now was perseverance.

I'd decided at the age of six that I wanted to learn to play the guitar. My gran took me to a show which had featured a guitarist and I'd fallen in love with the instrument. For my seventh birthday she'd given me a three-quarter second-hand guitar and a book of chords and songs. I'd had to learn almost completely by myself because my mother wasn't interested in paying for guitar lessons. She said she never had enough money but that hadn't stopped her from going out to movies whenever she wanted to. One of her boyfriends, Ryan, had been able to play and had shown me a few things. So I knew from experience, you can do anything if you set your mind to it.

"That's right," I said. "Practise that a few times a day, as well as the scales I showed you."

"Ow! My fingers hurt!" She blew on her reddened fingertips.

"You don't get any pleasure without some pain," I told her. "You're doing fine."

I glanced across at Jill who was seeing to Tamsyn. I felt so much safer with Lynne since Jill and I got it together. Jill was like a shield against Lynne's power. I could enjoy both of them now, I could bask in the warmth of these two women.

Lynne put the guitar away. "Your turn," she said. "When can I show you how to make your first pot?"

"Let's get you going first. There's no rush." It was Jill I was thinking of. I couldn't push this too far. There would definitely be repercussions.

Later that day after my lunch-time slot, I found myself playing with a lump of clay, squeezing it through my fingers, flattening it between my hands, watching it take on my imprint. I don't know what to do with this stuff, I thought. It's as though it's waiting for something to happen, for me to make a decision.

"What are you making?" Jill had come up behind me.

"I don't know." I looked at her, her dark eyes, the

line of her jaw. I looked at the clay. "I suppose I want to make something of my life."

She sat down next to me. "Yeah?"

"Sometimes everything seems to be out of control, like everything's just happening to me. My mother leaving, taking on Kevin, coming to Knysna, getting this job. I didn't really plan any of it."

She looked at me daringly. "What about us?"

"Yeah. Well, I suppose . . . I mean, I saw you in the library and I wanted to meet you."

"So this isn't just about child care?"

I stared at her for a moment, then I laughed. "No. I told you. It's about discovering your secret store of lollipops." I wiped a stripe of clay down her nose

"David!" she screamed, grabbing a piece of clay and smearing it down my T-shirt. I retaliated by smearing my hands over her hair. Next thing we were chasing each other around the shop, shrieking and laughing, looking increasingly like mud people.

"For goodness' sake, be careful!" It was Lynne at the door, furious. "Get out of here! You could break something!"

I was struck down by guilt, I was four years old. Jill and I went into the house to clean up.

"I'll get you yet," she warned, taking a face-cloth and wiping my face. She seemed unperturbed by her mother's disapproval, triumphant even. She wiped and kissed, wiped and kissed, until we forgot about the wiping and just kissed and kissed, the basin hard against my back, Jill soft, pressed against me. The taste of clay on her lips, our senses mingling and merging, her body warm beneath my hands, my hands moulding her shape, wanting her, wanting her nakedness, to smear her body with wet earth, wanting to roll and slide in the warm mud of her. But still, a small voice, "You didn't choose this, you're still four years old and out of control, you're squeezed tight like putty in the hand of life. You wanted to tell Jill about your dream, your life, you wanted Jill to understand about your need to take a step out into the world and into adventure."

"Good grief! Look at the time!"

A clock on the bathroom shelf pulled me back. I was due back at the hotel in half an hour and I looked like the original monster from the swamp.

I kissed Jill one more time. "I must fly. I'm late. See you tomorrow."

I rushed through the shop, apologising again to Lynne.

"What about Kevin?" she yelled after me. Kevin. I swung around, went back into the house and collected Kevin from Nompumelelo.

"Dirty," he observed, studying my face with approval. "All dirty."

"Right on, Kev. For once I've beaten you at your own game. Thanks, Nompumelelo," I said and raced out again.

I can't do this, I thought to myself as I galloped up the hill with Kev, the speed freak, gurgling me on with delight. I can't do babies and work and women and get enough sleep *and* find adventure all at the same time. Something has to give.

And something did give, my sandal strap and Kev and I bit the dust. I just gave up and lay there, looking up at the sky and cradling Kev, who was scraped and shocked and wailing, but otherwise unhurt.

"That's what happens when you live in the fast lane, buddy," I told him. "All fall down."

"Down!" sobbed Kev. "All down!"

Twenty

"What're you doing for Christmas?" I asked Anthony.

We'd spent the morning poring over the plans for the yacht. I wanted to start as soon as possible, but it would have to wait until the end of January.

"I assumed we'd spend the day together," he said. "Perhaps go and have lunch at the yacht club. Why, you working?"

"I have to work lunch-time. Singing Christmas carols, can you believe it? We're invited over to Lynne and Jill's for supper. If you want to." I'd decided that seeing he was letting me into his life, I'd take the risk and let him into mine. Just a little. Just to check him out.

He considered this. "Well, it won't be the first time I've mixed business with pleasure," he said. "It'll give me an opportunity to take another look at their kitchen before I start work there in the new year."

"I've forgiven you," I told Rudd the next day during my break. "I'm even prepared to risk taking you to my girlfriend's house for supper on Christmas night. As long as you're prepared to accept that the only bird in the room is the roast on the table."

He stared at me. "Well, for a moment there I considered reporting you to the Society for Protection Against Cruelty to Animals, but if it's true that you've taken my advice, I'll drop all charges. Is it true?"

"What?"

"You've got a girlfriend?"

I shifted uncomfortably. "Yeah. Well. Sort of. Anyway, I told her about you and she said you could come."

Rudd beamed. He wiped a table with his dish towel and gestured to a chair.

"Sit down! Have a drink! Tell me about it!"

Over his shoulder I'd caught sight of Jill at the door of the pub, looking anxiously around. I stood up and beckoned to her and she came and joined us.

"This is Rudd," I warned her.

"Hi," she said. She was looking stunning in a short sleeveless black dress.

"And this is David," said Rudd. "I understand you're making a man of him."

"Oh, shut up!" I said, but Jill was laughing.

"I've come to hear you sing," she said to me.

"What a blow," exclaimed Rudd, slapping his forehead in despair. "I thought you'd come to hear my jokes. Tell you what, I'll get you two some drinks, then I'll do the mike thing for a while to give you time to gaze dreamily into each other's eyes." He disappeared with a flourish.

"Don't mind him," I advised her.

She shrugged. "He's fine." She laughed at a couple of his jokes, which, personally, I didn't find very funny, it was the way he told them that got to people, the right accent, the facial expressions. He's not afraid of making a fool of himself, I thought. That's a kind of risk-taking too.

Mostly I was watching Jill, her face. Was this it? I wondered. This feeling that I'd like to hold her and protect her, was this the real thing?

I felt a bit nervous at the mike at first, knowing Jill's eyes were on me, that this was a performance that counted. But I soon warmed up and was pleased to see she clapped longer and harder than anyone else. Then a couple of guys entered the pub and I saw to my irritation that they were Jill's friends from the river. They spotted Jill sitting by herself and joined her. After that I didn't even look in her direction, but finished the set, then went to get some supper in the kitchen.

Rudd whizzed in and out to get some clean glasses. "I see you've got some competition," he threw over his shoulder.

"Zip it!" I was stupidly annoyed. The next time Rudd flew in, he had a message.

"*La belle dame desires votre company. Dans les mots autres*: 'Where the hell are you?'"

"Your French always was terrible," I told him. He tiptoed dramatically to the swing door, peeped out and gesticulated wildly to me to join him. "Zee coast eez as clear as a babeez bottom," he announced.

"You clearly haven't seen Kevin's recently," I told him as I brushed past him. Jill's buddies had left.

"Where were you?" she asked.

"Having a bite to eat."

"Aren't you allowed to eat out here?"

"You had company."

"Just Pete and Toffer. You met them at the bridge." She looked at me quizzically.

"Yeah." I couldn't help myself. My body felt cold, I felt as though I was drifting down a river out of reach of Jill, even out of reach of my best intentions. I stood up. "Well, it's time for me to play again."

"Look, do you want me to stay?" She was upset.

"Suit yourself," I took up my guitar. What the hell do you want? a small voice within asked me as I settled myself on the stool and tuned up.

Out of the corner of my eye I saw Jill stand up. I hadn't meant it like that, I just found it hard to trust her with other men. Now it was too late. I'd been mean to her and she was walking out, out towards the door, out of my life.

There was a sinking feeling, a feeling of drowning. I couldn't bear it if she walked out of that door. What was worse, Rudd was watching. I had to stop her, somehow. Luckily the words of a song I'd made up some time back came to my rescue.

"This one's for Jill," I announced. The crowd quietened, people were looking at me, expectantly. I saw Jill hesitate at the door. "It's called Babyshoes."

> "There's a view of you
> I can't get out of my head.
> And it's making me blue
> So I wish I were dead.
> Oh baby, the baby blues.
> Oh baby, my babyshoes.
>
> I love the whole of you
> From the bottom to the top,
> But there's just one view
> That wants to make me drop.
> Oh baby, you're too good to lose.
> Oh baby, my babyshoes.
>
> It's the one you show
> When you've turned away

'Cause I can't see the sun
And my life turns grey,
Oh baby, is there no good news?
Oh baby, my babyshoes.

Please don't misconstrue
What I'm trying to say.
I love your backside too
Not when you're going away.
Oh baby, I know I don't amuse.
Oh baby, my babyshoes.

So my baby blue
Give me one last chance.
Give me any other view
And a taste of romance,
Oh baby, my babyshoes.
Oh baby, my babyshoes."

The crowd seemed to appreciate it, but had I got through to Jill? She'd disappeared into the crowd at the back. My heart sank. If she'd rejected my song then she'd rejected me. It was my best effort. Suddenly I felt terribly embarrassed. I was behaving like Rudd in his worst moments. I was giving her my face to kick.

"Good one," said Rudd as he passed on his way to

the bar. "I couldn't have put it better myself." He was such a pain.

I made my way through a couple of songs and wrapped up early. Let the management complain. I just wasn't in the mood.

She was waiting for me at a table at the back. She stood up and fell in with me as I walked out. I wanted to say something, sorry, anything, but there was still this cotton wool fudged between us. I could sing to her to come back when she was at the other side of the room, but when she was right beside me, I could barely look at her. Anyway, I'd kinda said it all already in the song. It was her turn now. We walked in silence for a while.

"Who wrote that song?" she asked.

"Me."

"Really?"

I nodded. "I wrote it for you," I lied. Actually, I'd had Beverley in mind at the time.

Jill's eyes narrowed. "But I've never walked away from you before!"

"It's one of those possibilities in life. I like to have a song ready for every occasion."

Jill looked at me dubiously, then she laughed. "It was quite funny," she said. "You're weird, you know. A nice kind of weird."

"Thanks very much."

We'd reached the shop and I saw that the light was on. Lynne was working. I didn't want to see her right then. She'd forgiven us for the clay fight but I still felt embarrassed about it. Seeing Lynne would disrupt what I was achieving here. Whatever that was.

"Come up to my place for a while," I suggested.

"OK."

I made her coffee. We had to be quiet because Anthony had put Kevin down to sleep in his cot. What now, I wondered. Had she forgiven me my idiotic behaviour?

"I'm sorry," I said, wanting to touch her, to reach out across the divide but not knowing how.

"OK." She sat beside me, she put her head on one side. "You got a problem with those guys?"

I shrugged. "I told you. I'm a loner. More than two's a crowd."

"More than two men. I notice you don't have much of a problem when Lynne's around."

"Lynne's different. She's your mother."

"Don't you ever forget it."

I was shocked to hear her say such a thing, but I didn't have time to ponder it, for Jill had kissed me, was kissing me, was going to kiss me. As suddenly as it had come up, the wall came crashing down and I felt myself dissolving into her embrace. She was so gentle, so warm, she caressed an aching need in me, a need to be held and nourished, a need to receive as well as to give.

"I love you," I whispered, shocked to hear it. I had no idea whether I loved her or not. But there it was, out it had come without my having thought it through, it felt so good, so right.

She pulled away from me, her eyes on mine.

"Don't ever say that unless you mean it," she warned.

"Of course I do," I protested, wanting more. "I love you more than anyone I've ever loved before." Which was true, the only other person I'd really loved was Beverley and I'd never laid a finger on her. I covered Jill's face with kisses and lowered her on to my bed. She'd forgiven me, she'd taken me back. I decided that I loved her for that alone if nothing else. I wanted to tell her again that I loved her, but her warning hung over me like an axe. I must choose my words carefully, I must know what it is I'm saying. "You're so wonderful . . . You feel so good . . ." I wanted more of this, I never wanted this to stop.

"Da!"

I groaned and rolled over. Kevin was standing up in his cot, beaming with pleasure to see me. "Go to sleep, Kevin. It's night-time."

"Tinkle tinkle sta!" He bounced up and down on

his mattress, hanging on to the bars, chortling with excitement. Jill grimaced.

"It's like they've got receivers tuned in to the frequencies transmitted by the erogenous zones," she said. "Tamsyn used to do the same with Jethro and me." She caught herself and glanced at me. "He's my ex."

I didn't find that funny.

"Uppie!" demanded Kevin, trying to hike his leg over the cot side. I disengaged myself from Jill and sat up.

"No!" I commanded firmly, wagging my finger at him.

"No!" parodied Kevin still more firmly, wagging his finger back at me. This has to be the ultimate contraceptive, I thought.

"Ignore him," I advised Jill. "If you pretend he's not there, he'll soon lose interest and go to sleep."

I kissed her but somehow it wasn't the same. The spell was broken. I kept wondering about Jethro, and Kevin kept up a steady chorus of his favourite nursery rhymes and songs, none of which are known for their erotic potential.

"Dumpty Dumpty wall!" he bellowed with gusto. "Dumpty Dumpty fall!"

I gave up and looked at my watch. "It's late. We should all get some sleep." I picked Kevin up out of his cot. "Come, Kevin, let's walk the lady home." Lady? Had I blundered again? What the hell was one supposed to call females nowadays? Jill had something else on her mind.

"I'm sorry," she said, as we walked back to the shop. "I hope I didn't offend you, you know, about Jethro. That was quite some time ago." She sounded anxious. I put my arm around her and kissed her on the forehead.

"That's OK," I said. "I'm on the rebound myself. A woman called Beverley. Kevin was terribly jealous of her and wrecked the whole thing. At least you understand the difficulties of having a relationship with a small child in tow."

She laughed, relieved. "I can see that we're going to have to organise child care just so that we can have uninterrupted time together!"

I smiled at her. She was lovely; maybe I *was* even in love with her. And I would see her tomorrow and the next day and every day into the foreseeable future. Time was on our side. As I walked back home, I tried to remind my raging, surging hormones that there was no hurry.

Twenty-one

We were at the beach when we had our next fight. We'd gone down there for a couple of hours with the kids one afternoon between shifts, leaving Nompumelelo to help Lynne in the shop.

I was particularly frustrated as we couldn't focus properly on each other in case the kids drowned. The most we could manage was to hold hands and talk while we watched Tamsyn and Kevin investigating the edge of the lagoon. It's not fair, I thought. I shouldn't be in this position.

"What are you thinking?" asked Jill.

"I'm thinking how nice it would be to kiss you and hold you, without worrying about the kids. I'm busy designing a kind of goggles with a built-in periscope so that you can look over your shoulder while fondling your beloved on the beach."

Jill smiled. "I suppose this is why people say sex falls off the agenda after your first baby."

Sex. We hadn't really talked about sex. But my whole body felt drawn to her as though I were a magnet and she were true north.

"Tell me it's not true," I begged.

"I'm sure it doesn't have to be."

I wanted to ask her. I looked at her lovely body, at her belly, where a child had grown, and I wanted to know whom she'd let in, whom she'd turned away. And why.

"You're probably more of an expert than me."

She flashed me a glance. "What d'you mean by that?"

Any amateur explorer would've seen the storm coming, they would've been looking out for it. They would've taken down the main sail, they would've battened down the hatches. Not me. I pressed right on.

"Nothing. I mean, you've had a child and I haven't, like you pointed out. And you've had other relationships. Like Jethro. You slept with him, didn't you?"

"What's it to you whether I did or I didn't?"

I shrugged, alarmed by her vehemence.

"I don't interrogate you about your sex life."

Thank God, I thought. There's not much to relate. I could be an advert for safe sex. The closest I came to having sex was to get into a steamy clinch at a party with a girl I'd met only once and didn't even fancy much. I had to go home early and wash my underpants. Hardly the real thing.

"Jill, I wasn't exactly interrogating you!"

She was past hearing me. "You know, you guys are all the same!"

"What d'you mean?"

She looked away, upset. What had I said? "You think that just because a woman has slept with one person and has living evidence of it, that she sleeps with anyone who goes out with her!"

I felt confused. "But you said . . . at least I thought that you . . . from what you said about Jethro . . ." I started to feel angry. "*You* brought the subject up!"

"Yeah, I did. You don't know what it's like, living in this town, where boys think that you're fair game just because you've had a baby."

"I don't think that!" I didn't know what to think. Jill seemed so contradictory, so hot and cold. In the midst of all that my brain heard the warning. I wasn't sure that my body did.

We heard a wail from the water's edge, where Tamsyn had got sand in her eye. Jill leapt up to see to her. I watched her crouching in front of her child, intent and focused in trying to help her. I wondered about Tracey, about her having me so young, about her dumping me with my gran and dumping Kevin with me. Despite her ambivalence, Jill was coping better than that. I would have to be patient, that's all. She'd had her fingers burnt, she'd be more wary now.

Patience, I reminded myself. The hallmark of a true explorer. But my body disagreed to the point that I had to turn over and lie on my stomach.

"You're lovely," I told her as she rejoined me. That seemed to lighten her frown. "I didn't mean to upset you. And I'm in no hurry. We're going to be staying in Knysna for some time."

I told her about my father offering me a job helping him to build a yacht.

"That's wonderful!" she said, recovering her humour. I was regaining lost ground.

"The bit about the yacht, or the bit about me staying?"

She smiled. "Both."

"We should think about ways of teaming up. Single parenting is difficult at the best of times."

She looked interested. "OK."

"I think it'd be good for the kids, too. I mean, my mother never coped well with being a single parent and most of the men she got involved with were useless. I could have done with a decent man around, one who was interested in me."

She considered this. "You mean, you could be a father for Tamsyn and I could be a mother for Kevin?"

"Well, that's one way of putting it." I panicked for a moment. As long as she didn't think I was proposing to her. "It would just be nice to share the responsibility with someone else you trust."

It would mean that I could go sailing with my father on a regular basis and Jill could have some time off for herself too.

A thought struck me, something I'd been wanting to ask. "What happened to your father, Jill?"

"He went out fishing one day about two years ago and never came back. They thought he was washed off the rocks but they never found his body."

"That must've been terrible for you. And Lynne."

Jill shrugged. "They divorced years back. He had another family. In Durban. It happened in Durban."

"Oh."

Leaving, always leaving. Men and women divorcing, dying, cutting themselves off from their children. A sudden thought: what if I died? What would happen to Kevin? I had to live carefully, I had to make sure that I stayed alive for Kevin.

"Why did they split up? Your parents."

Jill shrugged. "I don't know. My mother was always criticising him, always being so bloody right about everything. She wanted a perfect man; instead, she got no man at all." She was silent for a moment. "I think she regrets what happened, mainly because of me. She's got this theory that if she and my dad had been able to work things out, I wouldn't have gone out and got myself pregnant."

"Is that so?"

"I don't know. I was wild and angry in those days. I didn't want my mother or my father in my life. They'd behaved so badly, so stupidly, I didn't trust them at all. So I went out and did what I wanted. What I thought I wanted. So I got what I didn't want."

"What d'you mean?"

"Oh, you know. A baby to look after, being tied to my mother's apron strings, her criticism for not being perfect, no decent education or job, no father for Tamsyn."

That was so negative. One thing my gran'd always said, you had to be optimistic about life, or it nailed you. I opened my mouth to say as much, but remembered what happened the last time I objected to her view of the world. Change the subject.

"And your mother? How did she cope with being a single parent?"

"Badly. She came on to the market for a new relationship at the same time as I hit puberty. We were always critical of each other's boyfriends."

"She's had lots of boyfriends?"

"Enough. Fortunately for me, Knysna's a small enough town for there not to be many eligible men around."

"Why wouldn't you want her to find another relationship?" That would be reasonable enough, I thought, thinking of Lynne. But then I remembered my own mother's attempts at pursuing men.

Jill was looking at me crossly. "What's it to you anyway? Why is everyone more interested in my mother than in me?"

"That's not what I meant, Jill!"

"Then what did you mean? She's had her life and stuffed it up. It's my turn now. It's not too late for me. But she grabs the spotlight whenever she can. I mean, she's practically menopausal and there she is making erotic pottery! What is she trying to prove?"

I felt cornered. I didn't agree with her, but I couldn't disagree with her for fear of fuelling the row. Best to bail out.

"I'm sorry, I didn't . . . I wasn't thinking. Look, I've got to get ready for work. Please, don't be angry. I don't know why everything I say turns into a fight."

She grabbed her towel and stuffed it into a bag. "Well, maybe you should think before you open your mouth. Come on Tamsyn! We're going home."

I followed her lamely to the combi with Kevin in my arms. Were all the women in the world this angry? Or did I just attract the ones that were? Then there was Lynne. She accepted me, she didn't push my face in the sand every time I opened my mouth and said what I thought. I found it hard to believe she was as harsh to Jill's father as Jill had described.

We drove back to the shop in stony silence.

Twenty-two

Next day it was as though we'd never had the fight. Jill was affectionate and cheerful and left me wondering whether I'd imagined the strength of her feelings. I helped her plan the menu for the Christmas meal and to shop for ingredients. I even offered to help cook it but Jill said she and her mother would prepare everything while I was at work.

We saved the presents for Christmas night. I'd bought a wooden duck on the end of a stick with flappy feet on wheels for Kevin, but he was more interested in the wrapping paper. Then he and Tamsyn got into a tug-of-war over a doll that Lynne and Jill had given him which ended in tears. We distracted them with food and opened our presents.

I'd bought Jill a silver chain and was relieved to see she liked it. She gave me a kiss for a thank you, in front of everyone. I glanced at Lynne, suddenly, inexplicably anxious, but she was busy putting the red carnations Anthony'd given her into a vase. I saw it was in the shape of a beheaded man and judging by his appendage, it was clearly one of her creations.

"That's quite a dream," I commented.

She smiled. "I like this one too much to sell. It's called "Carnal Thoughts". Thanks, Anthony. The carnations are just right for it."

Rudd's eyes were standing out on stalks. Then he recovered himself.

Jill quickly handed me another present. It was a plaited leather belt I discovered she'd made herself. It was beautiful. I hadn't known she had such skill. There was so much I didn't know about her. I'd been too dazzled by her mother.

"I keep telling Jill to display her work in the shop," said Lynne. "It'd sell well. You should see the thong and bead jewellery she makes. It's truly exquisite."

I looked at Jill, my eyebrows raised. She was silent, averted, defensive. Now was not the moment to push this.

"David, you freak!" Rudd had opened my present to him. It was a second-hand copy of *Sex Manners for Men* that I'd picked up in a shop in Cape Town and had kept specifically for this purpose.

He'd bought me a T-shirt with 'Trust me, I'm not a Doctor' on the back.

"Very funny," I admitted, putting it on.

Anthony had bought me a CD of U2, even though I didn't have a CD player. "You'll get one some day," he said. "When you're rich and famous. Until then you can look at the nice cover and read the lyrics."

I was touched by his gift and I wanted to thank him, but I didn't know how. I realised that since we'd met, the only time we'd touched was when he put his hand on my shoulder at the bus stop. I'd experienced such pleasure to see him playing with Kevin physically that I wanted to hug him, but I didn't know how.

"Thanks," I compromised and gave him the present I'd bought him. I'd got him a yachting cap. I watched him open it, watched to see how he'd respond. He looked pleased, but stayed in his chair.

"Just what I need," he said, putting it on his head. Then Lynne and I exchanged gifts and the moment passed.

She'd given me a small vase, simple, but beautifully glazed and I'd bought a capo for her. Her guitar playing was coming on quite well, but I was still avoiding clay lessons for fear of Jill's disapproval.

I was in the kitchen with Jill preparing a salad when I remembered my gran, how we'd go out into her garden on Christmas morning to choose a present there for the baby Jesus. She'd ask me to cut a flower with her secateurs and we'd put it in a vase, together with a lit candle, on her mantelpiece and say a prayer for all the poor children in the world. I'd loved that simple ritual. As I prayed, I'd look into the very centre of the candle's light and see a place that was very still and quiet and pale. And if I looked long enough, I could see the baby Jesus's face, right in the middle of the flame, looking back at me.

Suddenly I was seized by a desire. "Do you have a candle?" I asked Jill.

While she found one, I took Kevin out into the garden to pick a flower. I then put the flower into Lynne's vase and placed it with the candle on the mantelpiece. "This is a present for your gran," I told Kev.

"That's a nice thought," remarked Anthony. "I'm sure Tracey'd be glad that you remembered her."

A double take. "Actually I was referring to Tracey's mother," I said. "Kevin's great-gran. I'm not sure that flowers and candles are quite Ma's style."

I lit the candle and switched off the lights. It was just dark enough to allow the candle its mysterious light. Everyone was watching me, waiting. I felt shy, but having come this far, I wanted to go through with something, I wasn't even sure what. I caught Jill's eyes and she was smiling at me with such pleasure that it gave me the courage to continue.

"I want to take this opportunity to give thanks for friends and family and to remember those who are not with us today and those in circumstances less fortunate than ours." We stood in silence for a minute, then Tamsyn strained forward in Jill's arms and blew the candle out.

"Happy bidday!" she squealed, clapping her hands. Everyone laughed.

"Yes, Tamsyn," said Jill, kissing her on the cheek. "But it's Jesus's birthday today, not yours!"

Jill and I put the kids to bed, then we all sat down to a sumptuous spread.

Rudd was in good form. He got on to stories about his childhood and had everyone laughing about his experiences helping out in his father's barber shop. While everyone's attention was focused on Rudd, I found myself feeling as though I was sitting outside the scene, watching the candle-lit faces.

A mere month ago my life had been so different, what would it be like in another month? I looked at these strangers, these friends, this family, Jill, Lynne, Anthony. Who were they really? What of my old life, my old family, although it'd never felt like one. What about my mother? Where was she tonight? I began to feel bad. I should phone home, I should at least speak to Trevor. I didn't really want to think about it. This was what I wanted, this was my life. I still felt too angry with Tracey. Two could play that game, I thought. She's not the only one who can walk out.

A squeeze. My hand. Jill leaned over towards me. "You OK?" she asked.

I nodded, squeezed her hand back. I'd nodded to reassure her but inside myself I could feel the uneasy swell of panic. All of this could be taken away, suddenly, impossibly. It was too good to last. I wanted to tell Jill that I knew life wasn't this simple, but instead I squeezed her hand and nodded.

"I'm just going to check on the children," I said and left the room.

Kevin was sleeping peacefully, his angelic face wrapped in dreams. I bent over him and felt the smooth warmth of his forehead against my lips. "How can I protect you?" I whispered. "How can I keep you safe?" He didn't budge, just sighed deeply and contentedly. I sat for a while on the bed, hearing the laughter from the living-room, hearing the shallow warm breath of children sleeping, hesitating outside the door to my life, afraid to go in.

Twenty-three

The next day, Boxing Day, I had off. I lay in bed with Kevin, feeling wrecked and trying to coax him back to sleep, then gave up the struggle and read his favourite library book to him for the four thousand and seventy-first time.

"And the lion ROARED!" I read.

Kevin's little face lit up with pleasure and his mouth opened wide as he ROARED in unison.

"And the dog BARKED! WOOF! WOOF! WOOF!"

Kevin squealed with laughter. "Doggie!" he said. "More doggie!" So we barked and bayed until there was a knock at the door. Anthony poked his head into the room.

"I thought a whole zoo had moved in," he said.

I looked at Kevin. "It has," I said. "Give it to him, Kev! And the cow MOOED!"

"MOOOOOOO," said Kevin with delight. Anthony sank haggardly into a chair.

"I can't wait for him to grow up," he said.

"You think it stops? Just wait until he gets into

grunge. That's the ultimate wildlife experience."

Anthony raised an eyebrow. "Well, at least he can make me a cup of coffee when he wakes me up."

I got it. I swung out of bed. Coffee. And then? What to do with this whole beautiful day, stretching ahead of me with not a single bit of work in it. My mood of the previous night had passed. I had shut the door on Tracey and my feelings about her and Jill had been so sweet and loving to me when we parted. I was ready to live.

"How about coming sailing today?" Anthony was opening a door to me which led into his life, he was asking me in. Today I would take it. Besides, if I was going to be involved in building an ocean-going yacht, I'd better know something about sailing. I would ask Jill to look after Kevin and I would go out with Anthony.

Jill wasn't happy about it. "I thought we could do something together today," she said.

"Maybe you could come along," I said, thinking, I should ask Anthony first. "Maybe we can ask Lynne to have the kids."

"She's working. She's got this big exhibition coming up. She was like this when I was a baby too, always working for something more important than me."

I was starting to feel guilty, but at the same time,

I really wanted to go sailing with Anthony. I began to get cross. "Forget it," I said. "Sorry I asked. Maybe I'll see you later."

"No, it's OK. I'll do it. Go with your dad. I know it's more important to you." The way she said it made my hackles rise.

"No, I won't go. I didn't mean to impose. I'll tell Anthony. By the way, his name is Anthony." I never called him my dad.

Anthony shrugged when he heard what Jill'd said. "This is an old argument," he said. "Tracey and me used to have it around you. We never managed to sort that one out. Who's on duty, who's off."

"For goodness' sake, Anthony! We're not married! I asked her a favour, that's all! Anyway, she didn't want *me* to look after the kids, she wanted us to do something together."

"So what're you going to do?"

I shrugged. "I don't know. Stay at home and roar myself hoarse."

I was a lion pacing a cage, a dog on a leash. So much energy to be out there flying across the lagoon, yet it all had to be wrapped up and bundled away because I had to look after Kevin.

"ROAR!" said Kevin, climbing on to my foot. "Horsie!"

I had this vision of Kevin attached to one ankle

and Jill and Tamsyn attached to the other. I could die here, I thought, I could never have another adventure in all my life.

"Your time will come," said Anthony, getting up and making for the door. "You'll see. When you're a grandad like me, you'll be able to go sailing whenever you want."

He was leaving me again. I was one year old, filled with rage.

"You've *always* been able to go sailing whenever you want!" I yelled. "You've *never* had a child stop you doing *anything* in your whole life!"

I wanted to stop him. I wanted him to spend the day with me, to make it better. Instead he hesitated for only a moment at the threshold. A strange look passed over his face.

"You know," he said. "Maybe you're right. Maybe it wasn't only Tracey forcing me out. Maybe I'm just not cut out to be a parent." He turned and left.

A huge depression sank down on me. I unplugged the phone and made Kev and myself some breakfast.

"Banumnum," exclaimed Kev with delight, as I mashed up his favourite meal, a banana in warm milk. Life was so simple for him, it was about food and sleep and hugs. It was about not having to consider anyone else in the universe. It was about taking everything for granted.

Waves of exhaustion washed over me as I watched him stuff his face full to bursting, making hungry, satisfied little noises in between gulps. For the moment he'd forgotten I even existed. The whole world was reduced to a bowl of mushy yummy goo.

"Kev," I said. He glanced up at me. "Would you please try, just for one morning, to look at things from my point of view?" He stared at me steadily, chewing his spoon, a string of saliva coiling down his front. "See, buddy, you owe me. If it wasn't for me, you'd still be stuck somewhere in our mother's vagina, or farmed out to strangers, or an emotional wreck. You'd be abandoned." I leaned closer to him to lend weight to what I was trying to get across. "Now, I'm not complaining that you're standing between me and a whole beautiful day out there. But, considering that fact, as well as your collective debt to me for the past fourteen months, I want you to understand that when we go back upstairs, I am going to sleep and so are you. Sleep, get it? Doo-doo. Shut-eyes, land of Nod, dream-time, forgetting reality for a few hours. It's a kind of adventure, you know. Setting off into the unconscious, you never know what might turn up."

Kev threw his spoon on to the floor and licked his bowl. "All gone," he said sadly. "All gone."

Upstairs, it was clear my words hadn't sunk in. I managed to wrestle him on to the bed next to me a few times, but he thought it was a game and wriggled out from under my arm, shrieking with delight. Then he tried to get on top of me. I pushed him off.

"Leave me alone, Kev," I told him. "I'm not in the mood. If you won't sleep, you have to play by yourself."

"Horsie!" he persisted, climbing back on to me and jigging up and down on my breakfast.

"No, Kev!" I shouted, grabbing him by the shoulders and shaking him hard. "NO!" His face widened with astonishment, then crumpled into loud wails. I was shocked that I'd shaken him, shocked by how much I'd had to control the rage that surged within me, so that the shaking hadn't released itself into a worse violence.

I pushed him away and turned to the wall. I couldn't do this any more. I just wanted to sleep, to have a normal life. It was Tracey I wanted to shake. Where was she? I clenched my fists, my teeth. There were a few things I needed to say to her.

I put a pillow over my head to muffle the sound of Kevin, who was standing at the side of the bed, snivelling a bit and imploring "Da?" every now and then. After a while he gave up and I heard him tinkering about with his cars and blocks. I lay there, feeling breakfast heavy in my stomach, my body heavy on my bed. I closed my eyes and concentrated on my breathing. In, out. Breathing in, breathing out. Father in, father out. Mother in, mother out. Father in, mother out. Jill in, Kevin out.

The first thing I noticed when I awoke was how peaceful and quiet it was. Only the sound of birds calling. Peaceful and quiet. Kevin. Where was Kevin? I shot up in bed, expecting to see him curled up beside me. But no, he wasn't sleeping, not on the bed or the floor. Then I saw with a lurch somewhere in my gut that the door was open. But I'd closed it! I always closed it so carefully! Someone must have come in, taken Kevin out to play. Anthony. Or Jill.

I rushed to the door, looked over the railing. A little bundle on the bricks below, a little child, lying as though sleeping. A sleeping child.

I don't remember going down the stairs. I only remember my body, cold as ice, Kevin's pale scraped face and closed eyes. And blood, the only blood was a little drop oozing out of the corner of his mouth. At first I couldn't see if there was breath, if there was life. How long had he been lying there? He was warm. Warm enough. I pressed my ear to his chest and heard the soft, rapid thud of his heart, I looked and saw his nostrils flare with breath.

I scooped him up and ran with him down the road, fear splintering the ice in my chest. Please God, as I ran, please God. Save this child, save me. My throat burning, my legs too slow. Kevin's body limp in my arms. Please God. A sky above, too blue for this.

An elderly man stopped, drove us to the hospital. In the car, Kevin's eyelids fluttering, his eyes rolling back. He's going to have a fit, I thought.

"He's dying," I appealed to the man. "Please hurry!" Please God.

The car too slow, the world revolving backwards. At last, the hospital gates, the nurse. Gently I laid Kevin on the bed. Immediately she put a collar around his neck. His neck! I shouldn't have moved him, I should've got an ambulance.

The doctor, where was the doctor? She has to be called, the nurse said, putting a thermometer under Kevin's arm. A thermometer! But he's dying, I told her, he had a fit. He nearly died once before, please, please, get the doctor faster.

Kev's little face closed to me, to the world. You went too far, Kev. You went where no baby should ever go. Please, come back. Not being able to reach him, like standing on a river bank, watching him float away downstream, towards a waterfall, towards a point of no return.

After forever, the doctor. Young, too young, does she know anything about babies? She was talking while she examined Kev, shining lights in his eyes, feeling his head, limbs, neck, stomach, checking his lungs. Asking questions. I was trying to tell her what had happened; what had happened?

He fell, I said. I don't know how far, maybe two metres? I don't know. It was my fault, I was asleep, I'm not his real father, you see, I'm no good at this, I don't know how to do it, I never had it myself. Please, please help me, he's the most important thing in my life.

The doctor took a long white plastic hammer thing and scraped the end of it under Kevin's foot. Kevin's eyes opened wide, his mouth opened, he screamed. He moved his arms and legs, he saw me, he yelled his head off and reached for me.

I burst into tears. We clung to each other and sobbed.

"I'm sorry, Kev," I whispered into the precious curl of his ear. "I'm so sorry, Kev." The pressure of his little arms around my neck, his wet tears on my skin, his soft hot cheeks. I hadn't lost him.

The X-rays were fine, nothing broken. The blood in his mouth was from his tongue, which the doctor said would heal well and didn't even need stitching.

"But we'll admit him overnight to observe him," she said. "He had quite a fall and we need to be sure what you saw wasn't a fit that might recur."

The danger wasn't over, but he was alive.

"I won't leave you, Kev," I told him. "I'll stay with you in the hospital. I'll sleep right next to your bed tonight."

Kev slept a lot that day, much more than usual. The staff reassured me that it was natural after a shock like that and that the observations they took every hour were normal.

I sat next to his bed swathed in pain. If only. If only. Trying to remember how it was the door was open. It's my fault, I shouldn't have agreed even to live in such a place, it's obvious to anyone it's too dangerous for a baby.

Danger. It was too dangerous for me, being close to my father, allowing him in.

It was too dangerous for Kevin to have a nineteen-year-old brother pretend that he can be both mother and father to him. This wasn't a game, it wasn't an adventure. This wasn't something I could do only when I felt like it. It was full-time, a hundred per cent. It was another person's life.

At around four I phoned Jill. I hadn't felt up to it before then. She sounded mad.

"Where have you been?" she demanded. "I've been trying to get hold of you all day! And you left your dad's house wide open, you know. Anyone could have just walked in there and stolen something."

"I'm at the hospital," I said. "Kevin's had an accident."

She arrived soon afterwards and put her arm around me. I couldn't feel it, I still felt too numb, too contracted around the pain. "I'm so sorry," she said. "He'll be OK. Children fall and bump themselves all the time."

I looked at her, shocked. She didn't understand. She hadn't the faintest clue.

"I nearly killed him," I said.

"Oh, David, that's not true! Accidents happen all the time! People aren't perfect!"

"He could've died. I would never've forgiven myself."

"He didn't die, David! You have such impossibly high expectations of yourself. You do a better job than most people bringing up a child. You've had a fright, it was a close shave, but Kev's going to be all right. Don't beat yourself up over something that didn't happen."

I looked at Kevin sleeping. I couldn't tell her. I couldn't admit to her that I'd wished for the first time that morning, when my father walked out, that I hadn't taken Kevin on, that I could be free, single and not have Kevin hanging like a millstone round my neck. And my wish had very nearly come true.

Twenty-four

"Your mother phoned last night."

It was the following morning and Anthony was driving us home from the hospital. The previous evening, when he'd visited us in the ward, he'd been warm and full of concern. This morning there was a distinct coolness about him. He knows, I thought. She's told him. Panic tightened my gut. What now.

"You told her about Kev."

"Yeah. I told her. I didn't tell her everything."

"What? What d'you mean?"

"I didn't tell her you lied to me." He swung his bakkie into his driveway and came to a stop outside the shed. "I think we need a little talk, you and me." He got out of the bakkie, slammed the door and strode into the house without looking back.

I gave Kevin a hug. "We're home, my boy." I looked at the stairs to the loft and the ground where I'd found him lying the previous day. It seemed like months ago. "No-one's going to take you away from me, Kev. No-one."

It felt like going into the headmaster's office. I

haven't done anything wrong, I reminded myself. How dare he treat me like this? He was leaning against the kitchen counter, waiting for the kettle to boil.

"I should've known," he said. "There were holes in your story big enough to drive a tank into."

"You didn't need to know," I retorted. "It's my business, not yours."

He turned on me. "Why the hell are you so hostile towards me? Why d'you have to bullshit me, to push me out all the time? What else haven't you told me, David? What other trouble are you in?"

"I'm not in any trouble! What did she tell you? And since when do you believe what Tracey tells you anyway?"

"She told me that Kevin's your brother. Half-brother. Son of that half-wit, what's-his-name. And that you brought him to Knysna without her permission, or knowledge. What are you playing at David?"

"You know nothing."

"Of course I know nothing! You haven't bloody well told me anything, how am I supposed to know?" He was pacing the floor, looking exasperated. "Look, if this is some weird ploy cooked up between you and your mother . . ."

"She's not my mother! She lost the right to be my mother, or anybody's mother, when she pulled out on us!"

That stopped him.

"What d'you mean?"

"Tracey left us," I said hotly. "She went off with some man, I don't know who. Trevor wanted to put Kevin in foster care. You can't give family away!" I shouted at him. "Family is for keeps, for good and forever! No-one around here seems to understand that! They think children can be dumped when it's not convenient to have them and picked up again when the adult feels like it. Sure, children can be a drag, they can be in the way, they can upset the way you want to live. But they didn't ask to be born! They need all the love and caring they can get! And they need it from their parents, both parents and if the parents are too buggered up, they need to acknowledge that and get help and say sorry and try again. You get more than one chance, Anthony, but if you keep passing them up, the door closes."

"I thought we were talking about Tracey," he said defensively.

"Oh, it's easy for you to point fingers at Tracey, or me, or Trevor. It's easy for us all to look at other people's problems and never consider our own. Well, yesterday, I had my face rubbed in it, Anthony. I nearly killed my own child!"

Hot tears pricked at my eyes but I was beyond caring. Kevin was looking at me in astonishment. He toddled over and offered me his soggy chewed-on rusk.

"Ta," he suggested, looking concerned. That really did it. I scooped him up and hugged him, tears streaming down my face.

Anthony came over and sat beside me. I felt his hesitancy, his awkwardness. "Why didn't you tell me all this? When you first came to Knysna."

I sniffed, not wanting to look at him, hating his sympathy. "I didn't trust you. You were never there for me. You didn't even like your own kid enough, why would you want to help a child of Tracey's?" I was getting rusk in my hair. Kev wriggled out of my grasp and offered the remains of it to Anthony.

"He's trying to get us to make up," observed Anthony. He looked at me, then at his hands. "Is it possible to do that?"

I shrugged. He was making an effort, but something in me still hung back. "What else did Tracey say?"

"She's on her way to Knysna." He looked at his watch. "She'll get here in about two hours' time."

I was due to play at the hotel that lunch-time, but I phoned and explained to the management that my child had had an accident and I couldn't make it. Then I phoned Rudd.

"How's the little chappie today?" he wanted to know.

"He's just got a couple of scrapes and bruises. Otherwise he's fine. But Tracey's coming to Knysna. She's going to take him away, Rudd."

"You reckon?"

"I know what she'll say. How could I do such I thing, why didn't I phone? I didn't look after him properly, look what's happened. Etcetera, etcetera. I don't know what to do."

"I'll have the getaway car ready at your place in five minutes," he offered. But it wasn't funny. He didn't really know what to say to me. He couldn't possibly know about the pain that sat in my gut. Tracey.

My mother. I'd loved her so much, but she'd fallen off the pedestal. I'd lost my father so very long ago, then my mother and now I was going to lose Kev. I wanted to talk to her first, before she saw Kev. I didn't want us to fight in front of him, so I told Anthony I'd be down at the lagoon when she arrived, he could send her there. First I dropped Kevin off with Nompumelelo.

I didn't want to speak to anyone, I wanted to be by myself for a while, but Lynne intercepted me as I went through the shop. Jill wasn't around.

"What a hell of a thing to go through," she said. "You OK?"

It was the first time anyone had considered me in all of this. I shrugged. I couldn't really tell her what I was feeling. I was too afraid of crying.

"I remember when Jill was about two, she fell off the top of a slide," she continued. "She stopped breathing for a moment, out of shock. I thought she was dead. It was a terrible moment."

I wanted to ask her, why then wasn't Jill more central in her life? Why was she more interested in her work than in Jill when she was a child? People were always leaving, turning their backs on their children, closing their eyes. No, I didn't trust her either.

I nodded. "I must go," I said.

The lagoon was still and silvery, with the railway bridge and the hills on the far shore reflected in its waters. I walked out on to one of the jetties and sat at the end. I wondered what the hell I was going to do next.

My rash wish was still trying to make itself true. I couldn't imagine life without Kevin now, he and I belonged together, we understood each other. I would worry to death about him in the care of my mother. At least I'd had my gran. I couldn't contemplate going back to live with my mother, not after everything that had happened. How to make Tracey see sense, how to bargain with her. She was impossible unless things were going her way.

The stillness was swept away by the hoot and chug of the train as it made its way out of the railway station. Kevin loved that train, a real steam engine, with its shiny brass fittings, snorting and smoking and steaming like some mechanical dragon. I'd promised him a ride on it one day. Now that didn't seem possible, unless I could persuade Tracey to stay a while. I would take him the next day. That was the least I could do. The hotel management would no doubt complain, but that was too bad. First things came first.

The sound of tyres on gravel. "David!"

There she was, winding down the window of her car. I felt a sudden wave of shock, not because she looked so angry, but because she looked old, older than I remembered. I sat at the end of the jetty and waited for her. Let her come to me for a change. Let her enter my world. I wasn't going back into hers. By the time she reached me she was puffed up with rage. I didn't care. I felt stony, immovable. She stood above me and raved.

"What the hell do you think you're doing, David! Where is Kevin! What have you done with my boy? How could you just go off like that? I never could trust you with anything, you're immature, that's what! Trevor was right about you, you haven't grown up, thinking you can just go off like that, as though life is one big adventure and with Kevin! What on earth got into you! And at Christmas time too, when families should be together! You broke my heart, David! I was worried sick! Then to hear from your bully of a father, of all people, I feel such a fool, that you let Kevin fall off a balcony! You know how he's going to use that against me? Now you sit there not saying a word! Damn you, I'm *talking to you*!"

For a moment I thought that she was going to hit me, but she leaned over and shook me by the shoulders.

"You're not talking to me, Tracey," I observed. "You're screaming at me."

Thank God Kevin wasn't there. She exploded.

"I've had enough of your smart-alec rubbish, David! Damn you! You think you can do what you like, well to hell with you, go and do it, but leave Kevin alone! You know what I think, I think you're jealous of Kevin. I think you always wanted him dead. You had me to yourself all those years, then when I tried to build myself a new life after all the hard times I've had, got married, started a family, you found you had to share me. You always had it in for Trevor, driving a wedge between us, always finding fault with him! Well, he isn't so bad, you know! He's treated me a damn sight better than that father of yours! But when the going's tough, you come running to Daddy, as though he's ever shown an iota of interest in you all these years, not even a birthday card!"

On and on, a storm buffeting around my ears, while out on the lagoon there wasn't even enough wind to ruffle the water.

I can't say anything to her, I thought. I just want to get away from her. But she was blocking the way. How to stop her. I have to stop her. Push her into the water.

I could see it, the look on her face as she surfaced. I began to laugh. That really did it. She hit me, slapped me hard across the face. We stared at each other, both smarting, like strangers, like enemies. I touched the side of my face, glad she was hurting too and remembered how I'd hit Trevor, how satisfying it was to see blood. Tracey burst into tears and sat down on the jetty.

"Oh, Davey, Davey," she cried. "What's happened to us?" She rocked to and fro, sobbing into her hands. Some seagulls squawked overhead, circling, looking for food. Kevin and I often came down to the jetty to feed them; he loved to throw pieces of bread to them and to watch them squabbling over morsels. She was trying to reach me, I knew that, but it wasn't working. Usually, by the time she became tearful, I would comfort her, I would set things right and apologise and work at getting her back into a good mood. But that was over now.

"Why did you leave, Ma?" I asked her. A canoeist slid over the water as smoothly as the blade of a skate on ice. It was so much easier to be out there in the world, doing things by yourself, pitting yourself against yourself, experiencing nature, than to be with people and all the pain and disaster that entailed.

She sniffed and looked up at me, astonished. "I didn't leave, Davey! I was just having a break, that's all!" Stony, stony rage locked around my heart.

"Well, so was I." I looked at her steadily. "I couldn't leave Kevin behind. Trevor wanted to put him in foster care."

Tracey was shocked. "He would never do that!"

I shrugged. "He said he thought it best for Kevin. Until you decided you wanted to be a proper mother to him."

"I don't believe you!"

"Believe what you like. You know, Tracey, he has a point. Being a decent parent is all or nothing."

"The dirty bastard! It's so typical of you men! It's only the mothers that must bring up the kids, the fathers do what the hell they like! If they have to so much as lift a finger, they don't want to parent any more! It was the same with your father, David!"

"Well, it's not the same with me! You asked me to

look after Kevin and I did, as best as I could. Let me get one thing straight, Tracey, I did it for Kevin's sake, not yours. Yes, there was an accident and thank God he's all right. I learnt a lesson, but at least I learnt it. Whereas I'm not sure you and Trevor and Anthony have ever learnt anything from the mistakes you've made as parents! Face it, *you've* never really wanted Kevin! I told Anthony that he was my child, because he is, in a sense. I love him, Tracey."

Tracey stared at me, shocked. She took a tissue out of her bag and blew her nose. She sat still for a while, fingering the bangles around her wrist. She seemed to be struggling with something. I looked at her lined, tear-streaked face and felt sorry for her, not in the usual way of thinking that life was so hard on her and somehow I had to make it better, but seeing her as a weak, self-centred person who didn't even know that was what she was.

"Y'know, David," she said, "To be honest, *I've* been jealous of *you*." She wiped her eyes. "You're so good with Kevin and he loves you, he loves you more than he loves me." She sobbed for a while, quietly, her tissue getting soggier and soggier.

I offered her my hanky, stunned. I hadn't known this and I'd never heard Tracey talk in this way before.

"It used to break my heart when he cried for you when you left to go river rafting, and to see how happy he was when you returned. It made me feel so . . . inadequate. I never meant things to turn out like this . . . I always thought I could start over again with Trevor. I thought that having a child would bring us back together. But when it didn't work out, I got so depressed, I couldn't see that anything was worth the effort. And now, my biggest fear . . ." She bit her lip, unable to continue.

I waited, watching the seagulls bobbing on the water just a few metres away, screaming angrily for their lunch.

Tracey sighed. "Oh, Davey, could you even understand? My biggest fear is that Kevin won't want me, that he'll hate me. That he won't want to come to me, his own mother! Maybe I've screwed everything up too much, maybe I've lost you all, Trevor, Kevin . . . even you."

I couldn't help myself. I put my arm around her and held her while she cried on my shoulder.

"Come on," I said, helping her to her feet. "Let's go and see Kevin."

Twenty-five

That evening, Rudd cornered me as I came through the door.

"Well?" he demanded. "What happened?" We were both a bit early for our shift, so we grabbed a beer and went to sit by the pool.

"We're still in the middle of it," I said heavily. "Ask me when it's over."

"What d'you mean?"

"Well, Tracey's freaked out, so Kev's freaked out, so I'm freaked out. And we're all staying with Anthony, so he's freaked out."

"Tracey is staying with Anthony? I thought they hated each other!"

"Yeah. Well. They do. But Tracey's car died on the way up the hill and the garage has to order spare parts from Cape Town. They say it'll take at least a week."

Rudd chuckled, then he glanced at me, then he roared with laughter. "That's proof that God exists," he said. "What induced Anthony to ask Tracey to stay?"

I shrugged. "Dunno. Maybe he wants to finish that fight she walked out on sixteen years ago." I sighed.

"And Jill? How's it going with her?"

"She can be so kind and generous, but something isn't right. This relationship stuff is beyond me."

Rudd nodded sagely and sipped his beer. "It's easy when you know how. Let me know when you want lessons." He'd baited his hook with that remark; now he leaned back in his chair, waiting for me to bite.

I looked at him askance. "Don't tell me you've become an expert overnight, Rudd Williams." He raised his eyebrows. I gave up and took it. "OK, who is she?"

"She's the most wonderful person in the whole world," he said. "Fortunately for me, you didn't notice that because you had your head shoved up your own backside."

"Thanks, Buddy. It's really great to get some objective feedback from an insightful friend every now and then. Cut the bull and tell me who she is."

"Lindiwe."

"Lindiwe!" You could've knocked me over with a feather. If it was true, maybe Rudd was right about the location of my head. I hadn't noticed a thing.

"She thinks guys are losers! Especially guys like you!"

"You see, David, what you have yet to learn, is that this business is one of give and take. She socked it to me, then I clobbered her back, then I kissed her better, then she comforted me. Now we're on to round two."

I had to laugh. "She's rather nice."

"Now don't get any ideas, David. She's taken."

"For goodness' sake, Rudd, you're starting to talk about her as if she's property already! She's so nice, Rudd! How did . . . ?"

"How did such a jerk like me catch the attention of a dish like her?"

"Rudd! A dish is something you eat off!" But yes, that *was* what I was thinking.

"Yum! I'll have a second helping any day."

I shook my head ruefully. "When did all this happen?"

"In the kitchen. We ended up late one night washing glasses together."

I laughed. "I always thought you were a romantic!"

"You should try it some time. Washing glasses can be the sexiest thing if you do it with the right person."

"I'll remind you about that after ten years of marriage."

"Come on, you lazy dogs! The people in the pub are dying like flies from dehydration and sensory deprivation!"

Lindiwe came up to us and took Rudd's hand. From the way she looked at him, I could see he hadn't made it all up. My respect for her increased still further. She could see through Rudd's bullshit veneer to his heart of gold. I was so pleased for him, it made me forget my own troubles for the moment.

I went inside and sang my heart out for them.

I put off going back to Anthony's that night when my shift ended and had a couple of drinks with Mike. I was afraid of what I would find, because when I'd left for work, Tracey and Anthony were in the middle of an argument. It was like being back in my childhood home, the same tones, the same pitches of voice. I'd forgotten, but now it came back with such a rush it made me feel ill.

Everything is out of control, I thought, it was my recurring dream of careering down the side of a mountain in a caravan with no brakes and no steering wheel. It didn't really matter what happened to me. It was Kevin I felt worried about. If only I could protect him.

On my way home, I went past Lynne's shop. The interior was in darkness and only the display was lit up. I wanted some warmth, but I also felt afraid of it. If I took warmth, what would I have to give in return? Commitment? Jill was serious about us, but I wasn't as sure. She'd looked so hurt when I'd seen her that afternoon and I knew it was because I was withdrawn. But I couldn't help it, it was just the way I was feeling, I wasn't sure it even had anything to do with her. What made it worse was that I couldn't begin to explain to her what was going on. I didn't feel like committing myself to anyone except Kevin, it felt too complicated, too layered.

What if I never sorted this out, I thought, running my eyes over the display of pottery in the window. Would I end up a semi-recluse like my father, or a serial monogamist like my mother, unable to commit myself to any adult relationship for very long? A cynical side of me kicked in, a small voice in the background, one that said all relationships were doomed to fail, it was too difficult to live with another person for the rest of your life. What if that were true? It scared me to think that.

A belt. There was a leather plaited belt in the window and some exquisite bead necklaces. That was Jill's work, she'd finally put it on display, put herself on display. I felt a sudden rush of warmth for her, I knew how hard it was for her to take herself seriously.

I would come back the next day and buy a necklace for Tracey. That might cheer her up. Yes, that's what I'd do. In one fell swoop, I'd appease the two women in my life.

When I got back to Anthony's, I found Tracey and Anthony outside on the patio, chatting over a bottle of wine.

"Have a glass," he offered, but I shook my head.

"That'll be the one that's one too many," I said, perching on a step.

The view from Anthony's patio was magnificent, particularly at night. You could see all the way across the black lagoon to the sprinkle of lights on the Island and the Heads.

"Always one for moderation," commented Tracey, lighting a cigarette. "Where did we get him from, Anthony?"

By the sound of things, it wasn't the first bottle they were on. Usually that kind of defining remark would irritate me, but she was sounding mellow, so mellow she might at any moment slide off the patio and down the embankment.

"Dunno. Personally, I haven't found him to be moderate in the least. I think he's as extreme as we can be, at times."

Here we go, I thought. Now they're going to start fighting about what kind of person I am and whose fault that is. But they didn't.

"Extreme? In what way?"

"Maybe that's the wrong word. A fighter. I mean, look at him." They both looked at me. I started feeling like a drink. "Here I was, enjoying a quiet existence in Knysna and he rolls up on my doorstep and turns my life upside down."

Tracey glared at him. "About time too."

Anthony hesitated for a moment. I could feel the tightness in my belly. If they start rowing again, I'm going to sleep on the floor at Rudd's tonight, I thought.

"You're right," he said. "It was about time. You know what, Tracey? It was a gift to me. David gave me an opportunity to make up with him. At the same time, he's not making it easy for me. He's making it one of the hardest things I've ever done in my life."

He's drunk, I thought. Not only is he a no-good bastard of a father, he's a drunkard as well.

"Good," said Tracey. "Right on, David."

I stared at her. She's doing it again, I thought. She's making me a weapon of her will.

My father. For the first time I'd thought of him as my father. I looked at him and saw a middle-aged, bearded man with striking eyes. He's just a man, I thought. He's just a person who lives and loves and fails like the rest of us. But he's making an effort here. He's trying to say something to me in his own quiet, bumbling way.

Tracey and Anthony. I couldn't imagine a couple more incompatible than the two of them.

"Why on earth did you two get together in the first place?" I demanded.

They looked at each other. Tracey sighed. "It was those eyes. And the way he goes out into the world without fear. He acts as though he owns everything, as though anything is possible. That's also the trouble with him, though. He is the most arrogant, selfish bastard I've ever met."

I glanced at Anthony, but he was laughing. " I got hooked on your mother because she was so outrageous, so determined to be herself and say what she thought, without caring what anyone thought of her. It's sad and true. That's the very thing that I couldn't stand about her in the end. However, she's still one of the sexiest women around, you know."

I was expecting Tracey to explode, but she was sitting very quietly. "It's not true, Anthony. I *do* mind what people think of me. I mind dreadfully. It's a catch twenty-two: as a woman, if you're completely your own person, then people have no respect for you; but if you become what people expect you to be, you have no respect for yourself. Now I don't even know what myself is. Nothing seems good enough."

This sounded like a mid-life crisis to me. I wondered how I could excuse myself discreetly and go to bed. Anthony could handle it. The night was softening as the moon rose over the distant hills. It was late and I was tired. I didn't know how this was all going to end.

"What are you afraid of, Tracey?" Anthony sounded concerned and caring in a way that pulled my attention. These two people had loved each other once. I kept forgetting.

"I'm afraid of growing old alone and unloved. I'm afraid that I've pushed everyone away for so long, maybe I won't get an opportunity to make up for it. At least David's given you a chance, Anthony. I'm afraid I won't get one."

She was manipulating me. Something hardened.

"A chance is something you've got to look for, Tracey," I told her. "Opportunities aren't always something you're given. They're like food or water. You've got to go out and earn them."

"I've come all the way to Knysna, Davey. What else do you want me to do?"

I glared at both of them. Why were they making it all up to me? I didn't create the mess of their lives and I wasn't responsible for making it all right for them. But OK, since they asked, I'd tell them.

"Firstly, I want the two of you to behave civilly towards each other while we're together in this house. I can't stand the screaming and shouting that went on this afternoon. You're setting a bad example for Kev. If you're going to have disagreements, sort them out quietly."

They weren't expecting that. Their faces dropped open with astonishment. I began to enjoy this.

"Secondly, I want Kevin to be primarily my child. You two can share him, as his extended family, but I want it to be openly acknowledged that I always have been and therefore always will be his primary care-giver."

Tracey's mouth opened to object, but I pushed on.

"Thirdly, I want to be treated as an adult and an individual. I am not here to be bargained over, manipulated or patronised. I want you to openly acknowledge that I am not far off twenty-one years old, which, if I can remind you, Anthony, is the age you impregnated Tracey. I am not a child any more. Fourthly, you need to understand that Kevin *is* a child and needs all the love and care and attention he can get and, as his family, you are both duty-bound to provide it."

I was looking at Anthony intently as I said the last part, for, strictly speaking, he had no blood relationship to Kev. I could no doubt have rustled up a number of other salient points but that would do for the moment. Before they could say anything, I stood up. "I don't want a response now. I'm going to bed. Let me know in the morning."

I lay in bed that night, my body aching with tiredness, a wash of something warm and pleasant going through me. I had stood up to them both, I had stood up for myself. Although it was still far from clear how this would all resolve, that felt like something I'd needed to do for a long time.

Lying there, at that threshold between sleep and wakefulness, at the edge of the dreamtide that laps at the senses, the gentle pull towards the ocean of fantasy and possibility, I met my guardian angel. She stood at the foot of my bed like a shaft of moonlight and smiled on me. I knew in that moment that I had never really been alone.

Twenty-six

"When I asked you two to be civil to each other, this was not what I had in mind!"

I was shocked. My parents were behaving like adolescents. I'd woken up the next morning to find them in Anthony's bed together. What the hell did they think they were doing? It was so typical, they were not to be trusted. I glared at Anthony. I would have to remind him that Tracey was still married to someone else. What's more, they were laughing at me!

"Come on, let's go," I said to Kevin. Let them ruin their lives still further. I wasn't going to hang around to witness it.

It was still too early to go to work, so I wandered down to the shop where I found Lynne, Jill, Tamsyn and Nompumelelo having breakfast in the courtyard.

"Muffins!" declared Lynne, indicating I should take a chair. "Join us!"

"More!" insisted Kevin, leaning out of my arms towards the food.

"You can't have more if you haven't had any," corrected Lynne, taking him and seating him on her lap.

"I see I've joined the Mad Hatter's Tea Party." I sat down and helped myself to some butter and jam. Jill hardly glanced up. She looked sulky and withdrawn. I felt stuck between ignoring her mood or working really hard to get her out of it.

"Mad hats?" enquired Nompumelelo. She took a serviette, rolled it into a nifty cone and put it on her head. Tamsyn and Kevin shrieked with delight and wanted one too.

"How's it going?" asked Lynne. "With your mum?"

I shrugged. "That's not a question I've ever been able to answer."

"What's going to happen about Kev?" She looked down at him cramming as much muffin into his mouth as he could.

"That probably depends on which side of the bed she gets out of this morning." My father's bed. I wasn't about to tell Lynne that. Why couldn't Anthony get involved with someone sensible, like Lynne? She looked so beautiful, with her hair swept back to reveal witch's moon earrings. I didn't understand how these things worked.

"Actually, today I've come as a customer, so I feel a bit fraudulent eating your muffins," I told her.

"Oh, yes? Well, I hope what you want to buy is for sale." Lynne raised an eyebrow.

"One of the bead necklaces in the window." I wasn't going to give one to Tracey after her behaviour the previous night, but I wanted to indicate to Jill somehow that I supported her.

Lynne nodded. "They're beautiful, aren't they? I didn't make them." She looked at Jill.

Jill exploded. She stood up and threw her napkin down.

"I'm sick of you two flirting with each other!" She stormed into the house. There was a stunned silence. I couldn't look at Lynne. How could Jill say such a thing! Overreacting again. Attention-seeking.

Nompumelelo picked up the two children, one on each hip, then she stood and looked down at me. "You'd better go talk to her," she said. She turned and walked into the playroom. "Mad hats," she muttered. "Definitely mad hats."

I couldn't sit there with Lynne, much as I wanted to pretend nothing had happened, so I stood up. Out of control. Why was nothing ever simple and straightforward?

"I don't know what's come over her," Lynne scraped her hair back irritably. "Was it something I said?"

I shrugged, not looking at her, afraid of flirting with her. "I'd better go and find out."

I went inside and up the stairs. Jill's bedroom

door was shut. I sat down on the top stair and considered my options. It really went against the grain to do a soft-shoe shuffle around Jill. I'd been doing that all my life with my mother and I didn't want to get into that with someone else.

From where I was sitting, I could see the lagoon through a window. I could walk out, I could go down to the yacht club and organise to crew for someone on the weekend. I didn't need my father to sail. I could write this relationship off as bad luck, poor judgement and go on and find someone else, someone who, like Lindiwe with Rudd, didn't criticise me every time I opened my mouth.

I was rooted to the spot. Afraid to go into the bedroom in case Jill rejected me or shouted at me. Afraid she wouldn't see me for who I was. Afraid because she had seen into my heart, knew that I *did* flirt with her mother. What had she said? That Lynne flirted with me too! Was it true? Or was it Jill being insecure and jealous? Either way, denying it would hurt Jill more. Admitting to it would hurt her too.

What to do? I closed my eyes and saw myself wedged in a crevice, stuck between a rock and a hard place, unable to move on or to go back. My mother called this love.

My guardian angel. Where was she? I'll talk to her, I thought. Fill her in. I've messed things up, I told her. I don't know what to do. Please help me. I've never been shown how, I've only had terrible role models, ones that break and destroy and run away or cling too tight. I don't want to be like that, I don't want a life like that. Surely there's another way; if there is, I'm sure you know it. Please, help me.

She was standing in front of me, looking down at me, smiling. Then, as I watched, she went across the landing and disappeared through Jill's door. Time passed, but she didn't reappear. What's she doing in there? I wondered with annoyance. She's seen into my heart and knows I'm bad, she doesn't want me any more.

I closed my eyes, tried to will her back. Nothing happened. I imagined it all, I thought. Stupid game. You think you can sort out your problems by imagining spooks and angels. Jerk. There's no easy way out of this stuff. We're born into it, that's what and no wishful thinking is ever going to change that.

Still nothing. Well, I can't sit here all day, I thought. I have to go to work soon. I'll have to talk to Jill later, try to sort something out, make her see sense. I stood up, stood looking at her door. Maybe I should try. Knock and see what happens.

I walked to the door, raised my knuckles. Lowered them. Tried again. It was no good. I couldn't bring myself to knock at the door. I turned and walked slowly down the stairs. Then stopped. How to get out of the house without seeing Lynne. Then it struck me. I didn't want to see Lynne because I desperately *wanted* to see Lynne, not Jill. She had some explaining to do.

I marched down the stairs and into the shop. Lynne was busy with a customer, so I hung around impatiently, waiting for her to finish. As soon as the customer had left, I closed and locked the door of the shop, turned the sign around to "Closed" and pulled down the blind. I turned and looked at Lynne, at her astonished face, her beautiful, terrible face.

"You *did* flirt with me," I blurted.

She frowned a little. "I like you, David. I feel warmth towards you. Jill has mistaken . . ."

"It's not a mistake," I said, trembling with the effort. "I know it's not a mistake." I leaned back against the door to steady myself. She was on the other side of the room, she was a million miles away. It would be easier to say this if she was closer, it would be easier to say it if she wasn't in the room at all. "There's an . . . attraction . . . between us. I know it now. You know it."

She threw her head back and exhaled in a kind of half-laugh, half-release. "David, you're an attractive person. I would like to think I'm not over the hill yet."

A desperation seized me. Was she going to deny

it all? "You know what I mean! It's taken Jill rubbing my nose in it for me to see what's really going on!"

"There are always a million things going on! Focusing on only one thing doesn't allow you to see the whole picture!"

Damn this woman. "You know what I'm talking about!"

"David! I'm old enough to be your mother!"

She stood there, beautiful, defensive, unavailable, desirable.

"I don't care," I said. "You said yourself that real creativity comes out of breaking rules." I wanted to stride across the room, to hold her face to mine, to kiss her. I could hardly breathe.

She averted her face, she brushed a loose strand of hair out of her eyes. "Breaking rules only works when you don't break everything else in the process. You and me . . . It wouldn't work." She raised her head and looked at me full in the eyes. "Look, David, you have to trust me on this one. I've been in a lot of relationships and they're not easy. I don't want this to be messed up. We could have a fling and then it'd be over. I'd prefer not to do that. I'd prefer to know you for a long time."

I leaned back on a table. I understood. "It's about Jill, isn't it?"

"Of course it's about Jill. But it also isn't about

Jill. I'm too old for you, David, and in some ways you're too young for me." She saw the look on my face and added quickly, "I don't mean that in a derogatory way. It's just that, when you've seen a certain amount of life, it puts you in a different relationship to it. It's not like when you were young and anything seemed possible. It's tempting to believe you can just follow blindly where your heart leads you. With this, I don't feel so blind. I *know* where this will lead."

"You think I won't love you when you're old, and I'm still middle-aged, is that it?"

"You won't. I've made many mistakes in my life but this isn't going to be one of them."

I felt a sudden anger. "Then why did you flirt with me? Why did you tell me that anything is possible?"

She was quiet for a moment. "I want you for Jill. I wanted you to like me, us, this family. I didn't . . . I didn't mean this to happen . . ." She bit her lip. "I didn't understand what I was doing." She looked about her. "I should stick to making pots."

"Yeah, great. You mess up my life and Jill's and then you say, sorry, I didn't mean that, let's pretend that none of this has happened. Just look at this!" I grabbed one of her phallic vases and thrust it at her. "Is this the only place your sexuality expresses itself? Or is this the way you like to manipulate men?" She stared at me, angry now, silent. "Tell me!"

"I want something different from relationships, something that most men are unable to give, it seems. It's one of the things I liked about you and it's something I wanted for Jill, God help her, she's had such useless boyfriends in the past. I don't want her to wind up in a dead-end relationship, or alone, like me."

"Why are you alone? What is it you want from men? Are none of us good enough for you?"

"I don't like being shouted at."

"Yeah, well I don't like being used as a pawn in a match-making game."

"That was not my intention." We glared at each other. Was this where it ended?

I couldn't help myself. So near, but so far. "Give me a chance, Lynne." Let me prove that I'm old enough, sensitive enough, loving enough. "Give yourself a chance. Who cares what anyone else thinks?"

Jill, suddenly, at the door. Her face, pale and distorted with shock. She turned and ran back into the house.

Twenty-seven

Sweat. Sweat beading, leached by the sun, stinging my eyes. My T-shirt clinging to my back. The road to the top of the Heads winding steeply ahead, the burn in my chest, the stretch and pull, pushing the hill down and away. It was a hot day, with a light wind blowing. Not far to the top now, my lungs searing. Concentrate on your goal. No rest till then, no room for other thoughts, just the rhythm of the tar coming up to meet your feet, just the thrust away. I'd made good time too, it was only twenty minutes since I'd pulled on my running shorts and shoes and left Anthony's place.

Good time. A good time to run away from those greedy slobs stuffing their faces, from the hotel management looking at their watches, wondering where I was. A good time for running away, heading for the steepest hill around, forcing my body beyond pain into a place of no feeling, where the loudest sound is the blood and air in your chest colliding and there's only you, you and God and the sun at your back.

Not far now, I was almost at the top; but no, another bend and the road carries on, flanked by mansions. It shouldn't be allowed, these millionaires taking all the beauty for themselves. They have it too easy, their soft bodies in large armoured cars, the world at their beck and call.

A face at a window staring out, a woman's face blurred with terror, white with rage. No, it's locked in there too, even money doesn't stop the pain.

Just another bend and the slope eases up, as though I've broken through the roof of the world and I'm floating now, my aching legs swimming through the air. Down to the lookout point – look out! – a person could die here, where the earth falls a sudden thousand metres into the sea, where, on a clear day such as this, you can see the wreck of the Piquita, resting on the sea bed; so many ways to die!

Not like this, not with a knife turning in your heart, not in a mansion of chrome and glass, not in a little loft room you pretend is yours, but that belongs to your father anyway. There are better ways to die. Better ways to live.

Keep moving. Turn away from the lift and surge, from the urgent pull of the waves below, turn away, run away, just keeping my feet moving, my body somehow attached, my thoughts like shadows following.

*

"Wow. That's quite a story," said Rudd. "I didn't know you lived such an exciting and dangerous life."

"Oh, zip it!" I said angrily. "If that's all the support you can offer, bugger off."

Rudd looked at me contritely. "Sorry. I didn't mean it that way. Look at it like this. You were what it took to get Jill to leave her mother, cut the apron strings and go out into the world to seek her fortune. At least something good came of it."

"How d'you know it's good?"

"It's what she always wanted. You told me so yourself."

"You've got a weird way of looking at things," I told him. "I've just wrecked Jill's life, I've just proved to her that men can't be trusted and that her mother's a bitch. Besides, it's not going to be easy for her. Her cousin won't be able to support her forever."

"It's a start. You made a start and look where you've got. You've got custody of Kevin, you've got your father back and meaningful employment and you're on semi-speaking terms with your mother. Now those are achievements many would die for."

"You don't get it. I betrayed Jill. I'm a bastard, Rudd, I behaved like an idiot. And I'm reaping the consequences. I've lost them both."

"OK. You win. You thought you were the good

guy and you turned out to be the villain of the piece. Now what?"

"I don't know." I was seized by despair. I didn't want to be talking to Rudd about it, but it was even worse being alone with my thoughts.

"Put it this way." Rudd was making maximum use of this opportunity to wax guru. He made me sick. "You were a step away from conquering Everest, but you tripped over your own shoelaces and fell over the edge. You're still falling and it's a long way down. But you know what'll happen when you hit the bottom?"

I glared at him. "What?"

"You'll start climbing again. Only this time, you'll wear boots with velcro straps."

Jill left town without letting me see her, or talk to her, to try to explain or apologise. I felt so embarrassed by what had happened and I couldn't bear that I'd caused her so much pain. And I was furious with Lynne. She should've known better. She'd set it all up, then wouldn't follow through on it. Jill'd seen it coming but I hadn't believed her. But then, I argued, Jill had set it up too. If she'd been nicer, less angry, less dependent on me, then maybe it would've been different for us.

For a while I felt struck down, I felt ill in a strange disembodied way. It didn't take Anthony very long to spot my depression. Since Tracey'd gone back to Cape Town, he'd started on Lynne's kitchen. I'd finished off at the hotel and was helping him in his workshop. I was getting increasingly worried he'd want me to work with him and Vossie on site at Lynne's house. That just wouldn't be possible. I had to get out of this job and start on the yacht.

"What's up?" he asked me.

I shrugged. "Something hit me that I didn't see coming." I wanted to leave it at that, I didn't want to make myself vulnerable to him when I was already lying in the gutter.

"It's Jill, isn't it? Lynne told me she and Tamsyn left for Johannesburg."

What else has she told you? I wondered. I couldn't bear to think of Anthony comforting Lynne, of her taking him into her confidence. I had to get him to promise to stay out of it.

"It's not only about Jill," I said, hesitantly. "I also fell out with Lynne. So I can't work at her place."

Anthony raised his eyebrows. "Oh?" So he didn't know what'd happened. He got two beers out of the fridge and handed me one. I could see he was dying to ask me about it. "You don't have to worry about seeing Lynne. She's off to her exhibition opening in Jo'burg tomorrow. By the time she gets back, we'll be finished."

Even with her gone, I didn't know whether I could bear working at her place in the midst of those memories. We sat in silence on the patio for a while, watching the sun go down. It's so beautiful out there, I thought. Why can't I have any of it?

"Understanding women is like learning a different language," Anthony mused.

"Looks like you're not too good at languages either."

He smiled. "Learning a new language requires effort and will. And goodwill." He took a sip of his beer and wiped the foam off his beard with the back of his hand. "I suppose I'm too selfish for that. For years I blamed the women in my life for the fights. Then one day I realised it was me who didn't want to make the effort." He looked at me. "You've got to choose. It's not easy."

"Choose what?"

"Between the compromise necessary to make a relationship work and going your own way."

"I don't agree. I think you can have it all. I mean, what's the point of having a cake if you can't eat it?"

He raised his eyebrows, looked over at Kevin, who was unravelling a seam on his teddy bear. "You've already made a choice. You've chosen Kevin. That required sacrifice and commitment."

That was true. "Surely it's not the same with an

adult? I mean, a child can't fend for itself, you have to protect it."

"Sure it's different. I read a book once that said marriage is like a base camp from which the individuals within the marriage can set off to climb different peaks. It's a real paradox. How to sacrifice enough of your own selfish desire to set up a communal base together so each of you can follow your own selfish desire."

I had to laugh. "I like the analogy. Sounds a lot like having your cake and eating it. So why didn't you want to do that yourself?"

"It's not easy. When you're in the middle of a blizzard, hating each other, sometimes it's easier to bail out than to stick it out and see how you're not helping things. Fortunately for me, there are other ways up the mountain."

"Have you got there yet?"

"To the top?" He shook his head. "That's a life's work, David, with plenty of false peaks along the way. But I'll tell you where I'm heading next. Indonesia. When we've built this yacht, I think that'll be the next stop."

Leaving. He's leaving again. He's using me to build his means to adventure, then he's going to cut me loose. He saw my face. "What's the matter? Aren't you interested in the East?"

"You mean . . . ?"

He chuckled. "I mean, you're coming. If you want to." I felt light, I felt as though something rising inside me might burst. "There's nothing like a long voyage to mend a broken heart. I should know. After your mother and I broke up, I went on the Cape to Rio Race."

Indonesia. I wasn't even sure where that was, but I didn't care. I wanted to start on that yacht today, right now. I wanted to start on the rest of my life.

That night I lay in bed feeling as though I was on some kind of roller-coaster and my stomach still hadn't caught up with my body. Winning, losing, rising, falling. What next? The thrill of my father's offer was still rushing around my body. I was electric with it. Building the yacht would give me something to focus on, to take my mind off Jill and Lynne. But it would take at least a year to build, a year of sitting in Knysna with reminders of what I'd lost, what I'd broken.

Kevin sighed in his sleep next to me. I kissed his sweaty head and threw off the covers. I hadn't lost him. At least I hadn't lost Kevin.

Twenty-eight

It was strange to be back in Lynne's home as a workman, with Jill, Lynne and Tamsyn gone. Only Nompumelelo was there every day, minding the shop.

"How's little Mischief?" she asked. She seemed sad. Everything had changed for her too.

"He's settling down into the crèche quite well. But he misses you. Every now and then he asks for Lelo. I'll bring him to see you tomorrow."

"He'll also grow up to break the ladies' hearts," she said. How much did she know? Maybe she'd seen it coming before any of us. And what of my heart?

One evening I was working late, sanding and sealing, when Nompumelelo closed up the shop. As soon as she'd gone, an urge seized me. I knew where the key to the shop was kept. I took it and opened up. That smell, it reminded me of Lynne. I stood in the middle of the room, hesitant, feeling like an intruder in a space that had once been like home. I was mad, this was crazy. Better get out of here, finish the job, sail off to the ends of the earth. There was something I needed to do first.

I found a bag of clay stashed in a cupboard and pulled off a chunk. Kneaded it on the table, feeling the texture, silky in my grip, squeezing between my fingers. What now? I wondered. What next? This is a beginning, the moment before something starts to take shape, where anything is possible. What had she said? Start with an inner image, a dream shape. See where it goes. I couldn't remember any of my dreams, but while I was thinking, trying to recall one, I kept up the kneading and shaping.

Lynne. That dream of her handling me, moulding me. She was too powerful for me. It was a power I loved, that I wanted for myself, but I felt in awe of it. I looked around at her lovely work and remembered how kind and generous she'd been to me, how I'd thrived in her company. And Jill? Lynne'd stuck by Jill. That was the right thing to do. She could've left her child and gone off with me. It's what my mother would've done.

The clay in my hands was starting to do something. It was taking on a shape of something almost recognisable. It was a child, standing with his hands clasped behind his head. I don't know why, but the way he was standing filled me with energy, it made me want to do it better, to show more eloquently who this boy was, why it was important for him to stand clasping his hands behind his head.

I worked and worked at the clay, but my fingers were too large, too clumsy for this task, I couldn't get his features right and his arms kept sagging until they looked like a scarf draped around his neck. Well, OK, let them be scarf-like, let him tilt his head back into the loop of his arms, let him open his mouth. The effect was quite dramatic, he looked like a young lost warrior shouting for help, he looked like a woman with folded wings singing a lament. With a shock, I realised this was me and this was Lynne.

I was having difficulty seeing the figure, it was getting dark. I must've been working with the clay for three hours, yet it felt like minutes! I wanted to carry on for longer, but I had to get back home. I washed my hands and stood looking at it in the half-light, half expecting it to come alive, as though by some miracle I'd breathed life into it. I knew what I wanted to do with it, but was it good enough? Good enough for what? asked a kindly voice in my head. So I took the figure upstairs. It was the first time I'd been in Lynne's bedroom; it felt as though I'd invaded a sanctuary, that I had no business to be in there. But there was nowhere else safe enough. I placed the figure on a piece of paper on her bedside table and on another piece I wrote, "My First Dream".

I packed away the tools, locked up and went home.

*

As M. Scott Peck points out in *The Road Less Travelled*, life is difficult. It's the understatement of the year. He reckons that's exactly what we need. Without difficulties there would be no challenges. And we need challenges, whether it's rowing a boat around the world or learning how to work on conflicts in our lives. Only I reckon at times things get a bit too challenging. When that happens, it's nice to be able to take a break and go windsurfing in a forty knot wind.

The yacht will be finished in another six months or so, if all goes well. Anthony's teaching me navigation and I sail with him regularly now. I want Kevin to come to Indonesia too, but Anthony says he'll be in the way and Tracey's freaking out at the idea. I've got six months to negotiate this and to teach Kev to swim properly. Fortunately Kevin is crazy about water and when the wind's not too strong, he comes windsurfing with me on my back. No, I'll win that one.

I still feel bad when I think about the stuff-up with Lynne and Jill and me. I tried writing to Jill, but she never replied to my letter, perhaps she never even read it. And Lynne and I only greet each other at a distance and pass on. Except for once, when she stopped me in the street and said how much she'd liked my first clay piece. She encouraged me to carry on with pottery, but didn't offer to teach me.

It's true what Rudd said. I'm going to try again. I'm going to trust that there's a guardian angel waiting at the bottom of the mountain to scoop me out of the wreckage of my life so I can climb all the way back up to the top. At least I know more about what I want now. And what I don't want. And about who I am. So maybe Lynne was right too. I'm learning to trust my mistakes.

Rudd also stayed in Knysna. It's a hard place to leave once you're there. He and Lindiwe are going to get married and there's not even a baby on board. I think he's crazy to commit himself so young. I mean, this is for real and for life. That's what I think. But I wish them all the luck in the world. At some point, when the time is right, perhaps one evening when we're sitting together at the edge of the lagoon watching the sun go down, having a couple of beers, I'm going to tell them about guardian angels. Let them laugh at me, I'll risk it. There'll come a time in their marriage when they'll need to know about these things. It'll be my wedding gift to them.

Kevin's still not afraid of heights. I keep having to rescue him off the tops of bookshelves and ladders. Either he doesn't remember his fall or he's an explorer, after my own heart. I like to think it's the latter. He seems to know instinctively that when you fall off, whether it's off a horse, or a tree, or a relationship, you've got to get up, dust yourself off and get right back on again. I like to think that my son is brave and secure enough to take his life on and ride it right into the setting sun.

About the Author

Dawn Garisch has published poetry and fiction, has had a short play and a short film produced, and has written for television. She runs workshops on creativity and is a practicing medical doctor.

She is fascinated by relationships and conflict, and the power of images and the imagination, themes which she explores in this remarkable novel. She lives in Cape Town with her two sons. Babyshoes is her first novel for Simon & Schuster.